THE LATKE IN
THE LIBRARY

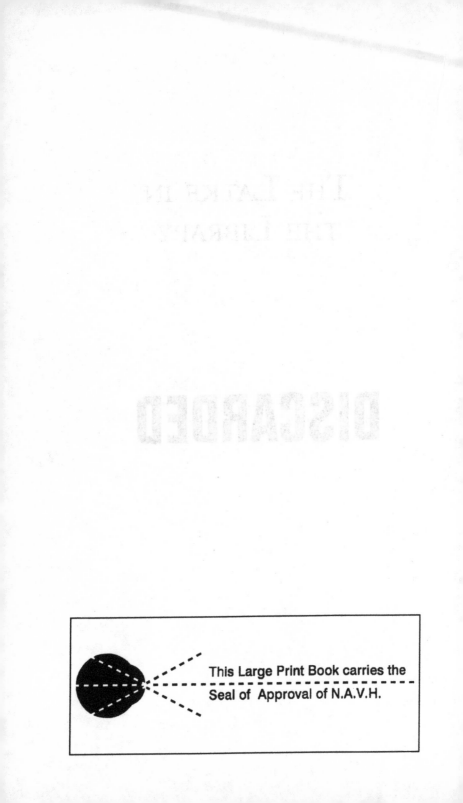

THE LATKE IN THE LIBRARY

& OTHER MYSTERY STORIES FOR CHANUKAH

LIBI ASTAIRE

WHEELER PUBLISHING
A part of Gale, a Cengage Company

Farmington Hills, Mich • San Francisco • New York • Waterville, Maine
Meriden, Conn • Mason, Ohio • Chicago

GALE
A Cengage Company

LIBRARY OF CONGRESS CATALOGING-IN-PUBLICATION DATA

Names: Astaire, Libi, author.
Title: The latke in the library : & other mystery stories for Chanukah / by Libi Astaire.
Description: Large Print edition. | Waterville, Maine : Wheeler Publishing, a part of Gale, a Cengage Company, 2017. | Series: Wheeler Publishing Large Print Cozy Mystery
Identifiers: LCCN 2017027172| ISBN 9781432839734 (softcover) | ISBN 143283973X (softcover)
Subjects: LCSH: Large type books. | Jewish fiction. | GSAFD: Mystery fiction.
Classification: LCC PS3601.S79 L38 2017 | DDC 813/.6—dc23
LC record available at https://lccn.loc.gov/2017027172

Published in 2017 by arrangement with Libi Astaire

Printed in Mexico
1 2 3 4 5 6 7 21 20 19 18 17

CONTENTS

PROLOGUE

"Here we are, Mrs. Krinsky. You've got one of the nicest rooms. It looks out onto the garden. We're very proud of our garden. I'm sure you'll grow very fond of our garden, too. Most of our guests do. This is your sitting room, and we do hope you'll be very comfortable. In that corner is your cozy kitchenette, for when you want to make yourself a nice cup of tea. Through that door is your bedroom. . . ."

The cheerful voice rattled on.

Agatha Krinsky allowed herself a small shudder. For too many weeks she had been forced to listen to the relentlessly cheery voices of nurses and aides and physical therapists. It wasn't natural for everyone in one's immediate circle to be so upbeat all the time.

"Thank you, Sandra. It all looks wonderful. Doesn't it look wonderful, Aunt Agatha?"

That was Agatha's nephew talking. Dear Sheldon. He and his wife Jean and their two children were her only living relations. It was very likely most tiresome for Sheldon to be in charge of her medical care after her fall — and now this. But did people realize how disconcerting it was to be in a wheelchair and to forever hear people talking behind your back? Not figuratively. Literally. Sandra Carstairs, the "welcoming committee" at Barnet Court, and Sheldon were standing behind Agatha's wheelchair, which was being wheeled by "person or persons unknown."

"Most appropriate it should end this way," Agatha said softly.

"What was that?" asked Sheldon, sticking his head round. "Did you say something, Aunt Agatha?"

Agatha turned her head — her neck still felt a bit stiff — and looked at Sheldon. She wished he didn't look so old. In her mind, he was still a young man with long brown hair and a reputation on the London stage as an *infant terrible.*

Now he looked like a middle-aged stockbroker. Of course, he still wrote plays. Vile plays, in her opinion. But he was treated with respect in the press, the way the critics do when you've outlived their predecessor.

She knew all about that. When she began writing her mystery novels, the critics ripped them apart, mercilessly. "Who cares who murdered Arnold Aaronson?" one of them had had the audacity to write. Today his name was forgotten, while her books still sold hundreds of thousands of copies every year. And, yes, apparently people did still care about who murdered poor old Arnold Aaronson, because that book alone brought her quite a tidy sum.

Sheldon was still looking at her in that concerned way the young, or youngish, assume around the very old. She forced a smile onto her lips. "I think I shall be very comfortable here, Sheldon. Thank you."

The features on her nephew's face relaxed.

"There are just a few more papers to sign, Mrs. Krinsky," said Sandra, who had come round to the front of the wheelchair. Sandra looked very young to Agatha, very young and very slim and very blond. It was the way airline stewardesses used to look, before the employment laws were changed.

"But there's no rush," Sandra

continued to chirp. "Perhaps you'd like to have your lunch first."

"Yes, I would prefer that."

"I'm in my office until 4 o'clock. Come by anytime until then. The dining room is on the first floor. When you leave the elevator, turn left. You can't miss it. Of course, today your aide, Karen, will take you to lunch and introduce you to the other residents seated at your table. It's a very lively group. I think you will enjoy them. Just press the bell when you're ready to go down. Oh, and we'll be having a little Chanukah menorah lighting ceremony in the lobby at tea time, for our Jewish guests."

Sandra left the room, leaving behind her a blessed silence. Agatha took a deep breath and exhaled slowly.

"It is all right, isn't it, Aunt Agatha?" asked Sheldon. "Jean and I looked at several places, and we felt this was the one most like a home. On a sunny day, your sitting room gets quite a lot of sunlight. And the closet in the bedroom is surprisingly large. Jean brought over the things she thought you'd like and put them away. But if there is anything missing . . ."

"Other than my own home? My old life? Let's leave the playacting for the stage, Sheldon. You and Jean have been magnificent. You've done everything you could. But it's going to take me time to adjust to being an old lady in a nursing home."

Sheldon sat down in an armchair, an armchair taken from Agatha's old home. It almost seemed like old times. "You're not an old lady, Aunt Agatha. It just wasn't safe for you to live in your house alone any longer."

"Because of one fall?"

"Five falls, each one worse than the one before. First, you broke your collarbone. Then you broke your arm."

"I know. I know."

"This time you broke your leg and hit your head and got concussion. You were lying on the ground for hours, unable to move, unable to telephone."

Agatha squirmed in her wheelchair. She found herself longing for

14

the days when one could simply walk out of the room, when the conversation turned unpleasant, with one's head held high. Even if she were able to wheel round her wheelchair in one deft move, where would she go after she left her room? The nurses' station?

"We couldn't let this situation continue," Sheldon continued. "And you agreed to come here. At least that was my impression."

"Yes, I did agree. You must forgive me. It's just harder than I expected. But I shall be fine, once I've adjusted. And once I go back to work."

"You have an idea for a new mystery?"

"Not yet."

There was an awkward silence. Sheldon glanced at his watch. "I'm sorry but I've got to get back to the theatre. I never dreamed the move from rehab would take so long."

"Neither did I."

"Shall I take you down to the dining room?"

Agatha shook her head. "I'd like a few minutes alone in my new home."

Sheldon walked over to the wall near the kitchenette. "Here's the button for the bell, for when you need one of the staff. You're sure you will be all right alone? I can call Jean and ask her to come over."

"There's no need to worry, Sheldon," said Agatha. She knew as well as Sheldon that Jean was a busy lawyer, and so it was hard for her to get away on the spur of the moment. "I'm now in good hands."

"I'll phone you later. And don't forget about those papers. They have to do with insurance matters. Jean looked them over and they are quite all right."

"I'll remember."

Sheldon gave his aunt a kiss on the cheek and left.

Agatha took another deep breath and exhaled slowly. Then she slowly looked around the sitting room. It was a strange sensation. The room was furnished with her own furniture. Her paintings were hanging on the walls, and some framed photographs were placed on top of a chest of drawers. But everything was in a jumble. The armchair from the library was placed next to the end table from the sitting room. The painting that had hung at the top of the stairs was now hanging over the computer table. The wedding photo of her and her late husband, Stuart, had always sat on the mantelpiece. And there was so much that was missing. But she knew she mustn't start thinking about that. If she had made the move when she was well, she could have chosen what to take and what to part with. But she hadn't, and Sheldon and Jean had done the best they could, under the circumstances.

And, really, the room wasn't so bad. The cream colored walls and carpets had the impersonal look of an upscale hotel room, but at least the room didn't smell of disinfectants. With time and pages from an unfinished manuscript scattered about the room, perhaps it would feel more like home.

A rather unladylike rumbling in her stomach reminded Agatha that she had been too nervous to eat much for breakfast. She had always had a nervous stomach before traveling or confronting a stressful situation. Now that she had arrived, she was pleasantly hungry. She reached for the button in the wall, to call the person who was to take her to lunch . . . Carrie, was it? But then she took her hand away.

"I am not an old lady," she muttered. "And this isn't the first day of school, either. I am perfectly able to go to the dining room on my own, and make my own introductions."

She reached for her walker and put it in position, so she could lift herself from the wheelchair. It was an action she had practiced many times while in rehab, and she congratulated herself when she did it well on the first try.

The elevator was near to her room. A few other residents were also waiting. When the doors opened they all got in. To Agatha's surprise and annoyance, the elevator went up and not down. She should have looked before she entered the car. But after lingering stops at several of the upper floors the elevator began its descent. It stopped at a floor to let other residents enter. The doors closed. Then the doors opened a second time and everyone got out. Agatha, who had been standing at the back of the car, followed.

The small crowd of four or five people turned to the right, and Agatha went with them. Then she recalled that Sandra had said to turn left. The others must be going somewhere else, Agatha surmised, as she turned her walker and her body around.

Turning left led her down a corridor. All the doors were closed. None of them looked as though they might lead to a dining room, which would usually have double doors, to allow easy access for a wheelchair, and be open during the hours when meals were served. But perhaps the place wanted to preserve a modicum of privacy.

There was nothing to do but try the doors until she found the right one. Upon opening the first one, she immediately realized her mistake. This was not the dining room. But it was a nice room. It reminded her of the library in her own house, or rather the house she had recently owned. The walls were lined with bookcases filled with proper hardcover editions. In the center was a fireplace that looked like it just might be a real wood-burning one, instead of one for those awful fake logs that some people had. If this was the case, and she could sit with a good book before the fire, a glass of sherry at her elbow, Barnet Court might not be so horrible after all.

Before she left the room, Agatha succumbed to the temptation to see if any of her books were sitting on the shelves. She made her way past a few comfortably old-fashioned grandfather chairs and a solid looking writing desk, and then she saw it.

On the Turkish carpet.

By the window.

A body.

A very dead looking body.

"Oh, dear," she said. "Oh, dear. Oh. . . ."

■ ■ ■ ■

Marsha Vane, the arts and crafts instructor, was just putting away some clean paintbrushes when she heard a scream. She supposed it must be someone who had escaped from the memory care floor. It happened on occasion. It was annoying, but not her responsibility.

At least it wasn't until the door to her room was flung open and an elderly woman stood in the doorway, trembling violently. Marsha rushed toward her, saying, in her most soothing voice, "There, there. You've had a fright, have you? Has one of Gerry's hamsters gotten loose again?"

Agatha made a great effort to pull

herself together. "It was not a dead hamster."

"I am glad to hear that. Gerry is always so sad when one of his hamsters passes away. But I don't think we've met yet, Mrs. . . ."

"Krinsky. Mrs. Agatha Krinsky."

"Why, of course. You're our new resident. You write mystery novels, don't you? I don't read them myself, but my sister was ever so excited to hear you would be joining us. My name is Marsha Vane. I do the arts and crafts classes, and . . ."

"Miss Vane, you must come with me at once to the library."

"To the library? Well, you know I would love to have a nice chat, but I am rather busy just now."

"Please, you must. Someone must stay with the dead body, while I phone the police."

Marsha looked intently at the elderly woman. "The dead what?"

"Body."

Marsha continued to stare. Then she burst out laughing. "You did have me fooled for a moment, Mrs. Krinsky. You could have been on the stage. I can see it's going to be great fun having you here. But where are you supposed to be? There are no classes during the lunch hour. Are you looking for your room?"

"I was looking for the dining room."

"And you got off at the wrong floor. It does happen, so please don't worry or feel embarrassed. I suggested to management to paint each floor a different color, so people would know where they are. But you know how it is. Everyone thinks they know best."

"Miss Vane, you don't seem to have heard me."

Marsha bristled. It had been a long morning. Although she loved the old dears, they did try one's nerves sometimes. Still, one did have to be patient, or one lost one's job. She therefore again assumed her soothing voice and said, "You want your lunch. I get cranky, too, when I'm hungry. This is the second floor. I'll take you down to the dining room."

"But I don't . . ."

"It's no trouble at all. The main thing is to get you seated at your table. There's Dover sole for lunch, with boiled potatoes and creamed spinach. I believe there's a nice dessert, too."

Marsha deftly moved the elderly woman toward the elevator, as she continued to talk. Agatha found herself helpless to protest. When they reached the first floor, Marsha handed over her charge to a woman named Maggie, who was responsible for the dining room.

"We have an excellent table reserved for you, Mrs. Krinsky," said Maggie. "If you'll follow me . . ."

"I would like to speak with the manager."

Maggie arranged her lips into

something that resembled a smile. "It is hard moving into a new place, isn't it? What I always suggest — when I'm asked for an opinion, that is — is to first live in your apartment for a few days. Make a list of the things that need to be changed or rearranged. Then you and the manager can have a nice chat."

Maggie turned and moved into the dining room. She was a sturdily built woman, not exactly heavy but certainly not svelte. Agatha supposed she was one of those 40-ish women who worked out with weights at the health club a few times a week in a continual effort to fend off flab. She further supposed Maggie was the sort of person who naturally expected people to obey her.

"A prison warden, that's who she reminds me of," Agatha grumbled, as she moved her walker forward. Her instincts told her it was better not to get on Maggie's bad side. Perhaps she would have better luck with her luncheon companions, and they would be able to advise her as to how to proceed.

Maggie had reached a table at the far end of the room and was standing behind an empty chair. Agatha reached the table a few minutes later. It was a nuisance having to walk with the walker, but she still felt too unsteady on her feet to do without it.

"Here we are," said Maggie, affecting a girlishly cheerful voice that was highly incongruous with her steely appearance. "This is our new resident, Mrs. Agatha Krinsky. And this is one of our very distinguished residents, Mr. Herschel Perlow." An elderly man had risen from his chair, and he made a slight bow in Agatha's direction. "Mr. Perlow is from Galicia. That's in Spain, you know."

"Ukraine, Madame Maggie," said Mr. Perlow. "There is a Galicia in Spain, but my Galicia is part of Ukraine."

"Spain, Ukraine, it rains on the plain just the same." Maggie permitted herself a short smirk at her little joke.

Agatha sensed Maggie didn't like this fellow Perlow, and that the feeling was mutual. They were very different types, if appearances weren't deceiving. While Maggie wore her straight blond hair pulled back into a severe bun, with nary a hair out of place, Mr. Perlow's wavy black hair (the black color most likely came from a bottle, at his age, thought Agatha) was parted down the middle and from there sprang out from his head on either side as though tossed by a never-ending breeze. On a younger man, a man about sixty years younger, the effect might have been romantically appealing, in an artsy sort of way. Mr. Perlow merely looked alarming.

"And this," Maggie continued, "is our dear Miss Eppel."

Miss Eppel looked up from the snowy white blanket she was crocheting. A faint blush crept over her cheeks at the unexpected term of endearment. After giving a slight cough, she mumbled something, which Agatha assumed was a greeting.

Maggie looked severely at the two empty places at the table. "I see that Mr. and Mrs. Bernfeld aren't here yet."

"I believe," said Miss Eppel, "that is if I'm not mistaken, Mr. and Mrs. Bernfeld went for a walk after breakfast. It is so nice to see a couple that still enjoys each other's company, after being married for so many years." An even deeper blush appeared on the elderly woman's face.

Maggie gave the empty places a sour look. "More likely they've gotten lost in the grove again. I'd better send someone to look for them."

"No need, madame," said Mr. Perlow. "I believe I hear Mr. Bernfeld now."

Indeed, a man of medium height and build, still spry for his age, had entered the dining room and was loudly greeting several of the residents as he made his way through the room.

"Hello, old bean," he said to Maggie, when he reached their table.

Maggie glared. Apparently she did not appreciate being called an old bean.

"Hello, old thing," he said to Miss Eppel. "Afternoon, Perlow. Glorious weather today. You should go for a walk."

Mr. Perlow shuddered and tightened the black woolen scarf about his neck.

"Is Mrs. Bernfeld coming down to lunch?" asked Maggie, icily.

"She'll be down in a jiff. Just went to powder her nose. Oh, there she is. Hurry up, Rubles, or you'll be in the soup instead of drinking it."

Mr. Bernfeld laughed heartily at his own joke, while his wife hurried to the table.

"Sorry, everyone," said Rubles Bernfeld. "You shouldn't have waited."

"We waited so we could introduce

our new resident," said Maggie. "Mrs. Krinsky, Mr. and Mrs. Bernfeld."

"Ronny and Rubles, when we're at home," said Ronny Bernfeld. "Glad to have you on board."

"Are you a former naval man?" asked Agatha, as they all took their seats.

Ronny made a gesture that might have meant yes, no, or "I've got a cramp in my hand."

"We're really not supposed to say what we did in the war, Mrs. Krinksy," said Rubles.

"The war?"

"World War Two, of course."

"Surely, after all these years . . ."

"What happens in, ahem, stays in, ahem," said Ronny, giving his wife a wink.

Rubles winked back.

"I'll leave you all to enjoy your lunch," said Maggie, looking very glad to go.

Ronny watched her walk away and shook his head. "I wouldn't be at all surprised if one day our Maggie unleashes her repressed disappointment with life and murders someone."

"How interesting you should say that, Mr. Bernfeld," Agatha said.

"Ronny, if you please."

Agatha preferred to keep a degree of formality with people she only slightly knew. But at this moment her first objective was to tell someone about the body she had found in the library. She therefore said,

"It is very interesting what you've just said, Ronny, because just a little while ago I discovered a body in the library."

Whatever Agatha expected, it certainly was not the blasé reaction that greeted her announcement. "Well? Isn't anyone going to say anything?"

Herschel Perlow patted down his hair. It bounced back. "What is there to say, Mrs. Krinsky? A library is a room. A room has chairs. Why should there not be a person sitting in one of those chairs?"

"I did not say a person, Mr. Perlow. I said a body. And the body was not sitting. It was lying on the carpet."

"It was probably Gerry," said

Rubles. "One of his hamsters must have gotten away again."

"It was a woman's body that I saw."

Miss Eppel stopped crocheting and looked up.

"Remind you of something, Miss Eppel?" asked Ronny.

Miss Eppel thought for a moment, and then she shook her head.

"I shouldn't think so," said Ronny. "A woman lying about on a carpet isn't the sort of thing you'd have seen in civilian life, eh?"

Miss Eppel cleared her throat. "Although I was raised very strictly, Mr. Bernfeld, I have not led an entirely sheltered life. I was on the financial committee of my synagogue's Sisterhood for many years.

Although one might not think it, there is much wickedness in a Sisterhood. One would be surprised."

"I'll say I would," said Ronny, "unless by wickedness you mean putting salt in the sugar bowl or some other prank."

"I mean wickedness. Real wickedness."

"Yes, well, that's all very nice," said Agatha. "I mean wickedness is never nice, but right now I was wondering what we should do about that body in the library."

"It was probably just one of the staff doing her yoga exercises," said Rubles. "I shouldn't worry about it, Mrs. Krinsky. But I would like to hear more about this wickedness, Miss Eppel. Were you referring to anything in particular?"

"Yes, dear. Actually, Mrs. Krinsky's mention of a body lying on a carpet did remind me of something. Of course, it happened many years ago."

"What happened?" asked Ronny.

Miss Eppel looked flustered. "I'm really not very good at telling stories, I'm afraid. I tend to forget the important details and jump ahead before I've explained why the detail I forgot was important. There, you see? Already I haven't explained myself properly, because of course you can't explain something you have forgotten."

"It is best to proceed slowly, with method and order," said Perlow.

"You mean begin at the beginning and go on from there?"

"Precisely."

"Well, let me see. As I said, it happened many years ago. I could still go about without a cane. And my eyesight was still quite good. That's how I saw . . . I'm afraid I'm already jumping ahead."

"Order and method, Miss Eppel."

Miss Eppel nodded her head. She then closed her eyes to better compose her thoughts.

THE LATKE IN
THE LIBRARY

"It's an odd coincidence," Miss Eppel began. "My story occurred just at this time of year. Chanukah. I had gone to a friend's home for the first night, which was a Sunday evening. Cheryl, that was the name of my friend . . . she died most tragically not long afterward. But I am getting muddled again. All I wished to say is that Cheryl served a lovely meal — roast chicken and potato latkes — and she brought out a really good bottle of wine.

I'm afraid we both drank a bit more than we should have, because the next morning, when the telephone rang, I'm sorry to say I wasn't as alert as I might have been. It was a married friend calling, Bernice Mansfield.

" 'Janice,' she said — Janice is my first name, Mrs. Krinsky."

Agatha acknowledged she understood with a nod of her head.

" 'Janice, you will never guess what has happened.'

"There was no need for me to try to guess, because Bernice was already continuing in that breathless way she had of speaking when she had some interesting piece of news to tell.

" 'There is a body in our library.'

" 'A what, dear?' I asked.

" 'A body. Isn't it too wonderful?'

"I really thought that might depend. If it was a daughter or nephew turning up unexpectedly for the holiday, I suppose it would be a pleasant surprise, if the house wasn't already full with other guests, or you weren't planning on leaving for the Costa Brava that afternoon. Of course, I didn't say as much to Bernice. One usually didn't have to say much when talking to Bernice, or rather when listening to Bernice talk. All I said, therefore, was, 'How extraordinary.'

" 'Of course, it isn't a real body. It's one of those dummy things. A mannequin, I think they're called. You see them in the store windows and on the shop floors, modeling the clothes.'

"I said I knew what she meant. 'But why is there one in your library?'

" 'That's what is so remarkable, Janice. Neither I nor Max knows how it got there. But you must come round and see it. I've already called a taxi service to pick you up.'

"I was about to protest. I hadn't yet had my breakfast and I was still in my robe."

Agatha noticed that Miss Eppel's cheeks turned a pale pink when the elderly woman mentioned her state of undress.

"Then I realized there must be more to the story. I therefore said, 'Bernice, is there something about this mannequin you haven't yet told me?'

" 'There is, but I must go, dear. The police are here.'

"Bernice rang off, and I hurried to dress. I was quite breathless myself after I heard the taxi honk and I ran down the stairs and out the door. There was very little traffic in our neighborhood at that hour, which was after the morning rush hour, and so the taxi made good time. A police car was still parked in front of Bernice's home when I arrived. When Bernice saw me walking up the drive, she flew out of the front door and came to greet me.

" 'I'm so glad you got here in time,' she told me. 'The police are still in the library, with Max.'

" 'But why the police?'

" 'You'll see.'

"Bernice led me inside, and then down the hall to the library. Her husband and the police inspector looked up when we entered the room.

" 'What on earth?' Max said.

" 'I had forgotten that Janice and I were going to bake cookies this morning for the Sisterhood Chanukah party,' Bernice said sweetly.

"Bernice had a tendency to tell little lies, even as a girl. It was a fault I generally tried to overlook, because she really did have a good heart. Most of the time.

" 'It is all right if I show my friend?' Bernice said to the police officer.

"'I'm about through here, anyway,' he replied.

"He was a nice looking young man. I would say he was about 40 or so, with dark brown hair that was beginning to be flecked with gray. His eyes looked tired, though, I remember. He moved out of the way so Bernice could show me 'the body.' I hadn't quite known what to expect, but I was relieved to see that at least the mannequin was clothed. She, or perhaps I should say it, was wearing a long and rather cheap looking evening dress, one of those satiny concoctions with sparkly glitter sprinkled about the fabric. It had a blond wig on its head — I suppose one does expect that if a woman's body is found lying on a carpet, it will be a blond."

The little group seated about the table made the appropriate reactions. Agatha, seeing an opportunity, said, "Yes, one does. And the body I found in the library this morning was also a blond. I really think we ought to call the police, before . . ."

"Miss Eppel is in the middle of a story," said Rubles, giving Agatha a disapproving look.

"Order and method, madame. That is the only way to proceed," said Herschel Perlow.

Perlow gestured for Miss Eppel to continue, while Agatha retreated into silence.

"Now, where was I? Oh, yes. The

blond wig was slightly askew, so that part of the fringe covered the mannequin's left eye. But what was most extraordinary was that a knife had been stuck into the thing's chest."

"How awful," said Rubles.

"Yes, it was," Miss Eppel agreed. "Because, you see, it was still smiling very sweetly. And even though we all knew the thing wasn't real, there was still something awful about the violence done to it."

"I suppose there was no need to telephone for a doctor, to examine the thing," said Ronny.

"No," said Miss Eppel. "But I believe the police did test it for fingerprints. Of course, there weren't any."

"And what did the police say about how this dummy got into your friends' library?" asked Herschel Perlow.

"This was another thing that was odd. There was no sign of a break-in. Nothing had been stolen. Nothing had been disarranged. In the end, the police decided it must have been a practical joke that someone had played on Bernice and Max."

"But you, you were not convinced?" Herschel Perlow's gray eyes shined with a penetrating light.

"No. No, I wasn't. There was something . . . It was only later that I realized what it was. But, no, I wasn't convinced. I was certain there was something more about this mannequin, something very, very wicked."

Rubles shivered with delight. "What happened next?" she asked.

"After the police left, the three of us sat down to breakfast. Max left while Bernice and I were still drinking our tea. He was retired, but he still went in to his former office a few days a week. To make a nuisance of himself, Bernice always said. At any rate, after Max left the two of us settled down to a really good chat.

" 'Have you any idea who might have done this?' I asked Bernice.

" 'I really can't think,' Bernice replied, almost wistfully.

"It was a bit awkward, but I did feel the question must be asked, and so I said, 'You don't suppose, dear, it was meant to be some sort of warning?'

" 'Warning? About what?'

" 'Well, she . . . or rather, it . . . was a blond.'

"Bernice looked puzzled. Then she laughed so hard some tea spilled out of her cup.

" 'You mean, Max might be . . .' Bernice laughed some more. Then she grew serious and said, 'What is so unnerving is to think someone entered our home without our knowing it.'

" 'You and Max were at home last night?'

" 'No, we were invited to dine at Dorothy and Isidore Millers' home. Isidore didn't look at all well. He said it was only a touch of the flu, but I wonder.'

" 'Did you go there right after candle lighting?'

" 'In a way, but you know how it is the first night of Chanukah. I couldn't remember where I had put the olive oil — we use oil and not candles, you know — and then Max tripped over the little end table where we had set up the menorah and the whole thing crashed to the ground and the glass cups for holding the oil shattered, so we had to bring out new ones. Then the wick wouldn't light. And I noticed there was blood dribbling down Max's hand and getting onto his shirt cuff. One of the shards of glass cut him, I suppose. So we had to fix up his hand and Max went to change his shirt. By that time, it was very late. But this time, Max was able to light the menorah. Afterward, I dashed to the kitchen to get the cookies I had baked for dessert. You remember, Janice, those Chanukah cookie cutters I have — the ones that were my mother's?'

"I assured Bernice I remembered the cookie cutters."

" 'Then we went to the Millers,' Bernice continued. 'I suppose you'll want to know who else was there, besides us and Dorothy and Isidore. There were also Edith and Abe, and Molly and Irving, and Bella and Sam . . . Bella and Sam came late. Bella was just getting over the flu, she said. It seems that she and Sam weren't expected to come. When they did turn up, it was awkward.'

"I knew all of these people, from synagogue," Miss Eppel explained to the others. "It was general knowledge that the four Miller brothers — Isidore, Abe, Irving and Sam — and their wives got together on Sunday nights for dinner. Afterward, the men played poker while the ladies played mahjong. It was also generally known that the brothers were business partners. They had owned a jewelry shop for decades. Isidore ran the business end of things, while Abe was the one who dealt with the customers. Irving did the watch and jewelry repairs, and Sam . . . Well, as the youngest Sam was always spoiled as a child and he never grew up entirely."

"He was a ne'er-do-well, you mean?" asked Ronny.

"I'm sure he contributed something to the running of the shop," replied Miss Eppel very primly.

"But the brothers quarreled?"

"Yes, although it wasn't about Sam, oddly enough. Irving Miller wanted to retire. His eyes weren't as sharp as they used to be, and it was getting harder for him to do the repairs. He had cataracts, I think."

Agatha might have mentioned something about her own problem with cataracts at this point. But she preferred, instead, for Miss Eppel to finish her story so that Agatha could turn the conversation back to her own problem with a body.

"So this Irving Miller wished to retire," said Herschel Perlow. "A reasonable request. Why did the other three brothers not buy him out and let him go?"

Miss Eppel made a few noises, suggesting she needed to clear her throat of something disagreeable. "That is what Abe suggested. But Isidore said it was impossible, financially. The business hadn't the money to buy anyone out, or let any of them retire." She then turned a trifle pink. "I only knew all this because Edith — she's Abe's wife — was a trifle indiscreet at one of the Sisterhood meetings."

"So it was Isidore who was the real ne'er-do-well," said Ronny. "Fiddling with the books, I suppose." Ronny gave the group a knowing look.

Agatha wondered what sort of business Ronny had been in, after "the war." He didn't have the suave look of someone who had been a barrister or a financier in the City. But to afford Barnet Court, one had to have a sizeable bank account.

"Of course, no one knew for certain," Miss Eppel protested.

"But there were ill feelings?" asked Rubles, eagerly.

A little too eagerly, in Agatha's opinion. Really, these people were too much like bloodhounds on the scent. It was as though they were detective story writers, too, the way they seized upon every detail with delight. Agatha wasn't at all like that. When she wasn't writing, she preferred to let her mind rest and let conversations drift around her, like gentle waves lapping about the shore.

"The eternal struggle," Perlow said, with satisfaction. "Brother pitted against brother. It goes back to the Garden of Eden and the brothers Cain and Abel. You mystery writers owe much to *le bon Dieu,* do you not, Madame Agatha? There are many first-rate plots in the Bible."

Agatha felt she was starting to

detest the little Hungarian or Ukrainian or whatever he was. She could not for the life of her understand why he sprinkled his comments with French words. It was so affected. And to suggest she needed help from books to think up her plots! It was really too much.

"But I hope I didn't mislead you when I mentioned the suspicions about Isidore," Miss Eppel was saying. "We only found out about that afterward."

"Then let us go back to the evening of the dinner party," suggested Perlow. "The others were already at dinner, when Bella and Sam Miller arrived?"

"As you will recall, Bernice and

her husband Max arrived late, because of the accident with the menorah. So they arrived at the same time as Bella and Sam. According to Bernice, there was an awkward moment at the door. Of course, Dorothy had set the table for eight, and not ten. And then there would be awkwardness after dinner, because only four ladies could play mahjong at a time."

"You could split up two and three, if Dorothy had two sets," said Rubles.

"I don't think she did have an extra set, dear. But Dorothy needn't have worried, because Bella and Sam left after the soup. Bella said she was feeling feverish again and wanted to go home. I believe it was Molly who said Bella shouldn't have come in the first place and spread her germs, if she was still ill. Molly was always very careful about her health. Then Bella said, 'I only came to bring the latkes.' Did I mention that Bella had brought a plate of latkes with her? Bernice noticed it because she smelled them while they were waiting on the doorstep."

"And Bernice had brought the cookies," said Ronny, with smug satisfaction. "We are paying attention, Miss Eppel, have no fear about that."

Miss Eppel looked flustered. She preferred not to be the center of attention. But because she knew how irritating it was to begin a story and not finish it, she continued. "So Bella and Sam left. While the ladies were clearing the soup bowls and helping Dorothy serve the next course, Dorothy said, 'I wonder where the latkes have gone to. I put Bella's latkes in the pan with mine and I'm sure I put the pan in the oven to keep the latkes warm.' Bernice and the others begin to hunt around the kitchen. The plate that Bella had returned was there, but it was empty. The pan with the latkes was nowhere in sight.

" 'It doesn't matter,' Molly said. 'We shouldn't eat them, anyway. All that oil is bad for the figure and the heart.'

Perlow gave a disapproving cluck.

" 'And what about the stomach?' I would have said to this Madame Molly, if I had been there. The stomach also has its rights, and that includes potato pancakes fried in oil and served piping hot on Chanukah."

"I, too, believe that once a year can't do much harm," Miss Eppel agreed. "Apparently so did some of the gentlemen, because Dorothy had to call a sister of hers and ask if she had any spare latkes. The sister did, and so Dorothy took the car to pick them up."

"Aha!" said Herschel Perlow. "We now arrive at the decisive moment, if I am not mistaken. What time was this?"

Miss Eppel considered. "If they'd

already lit the menorah and arrived at the Millers and had a cocktail before dinner and had their soup, I suppose it must have been around 6:00 or 6:30. Nightfall is so early in the winter."

"Did anyone else leave the house while Madame Dorothy was gone?"

"And how long was she gone?" asked Ronny.

"According to Bernice — but I must tell you that Bernice, although she has many good qualities, isn't always so aware of the time. She did tell me, though, that she was sure Dorothy must have been away at least a half hour, maybe more. As for who else left the house, Bernice mentioned she couldn't remember if she had locked the front door and so she wondered if Max would mind driving back to their home to check. But he was in a discussion about something with Abe, and he didn't want to leave in the middle. Bernice said she'd drive, but she didn't like to drive at night and Max insisted she was being foolish. They always locked the door when they went out, so why should this night be different?"

"So neither Bernice nor Max left?" asked Rubles.

"No."

"So they're out of it," said Ronny.

"And the others?" asked Perlow.

"You see, it was hard for Bernice to know. Everyone scattered, in a way. As I said, Max and Abe went back to the living room and had another cocktail while they talked. Bernice thought that Isidore might have gone to the TV room to listen to the news, because at one point she noticed the TV was on."

"But she didn't go to the room to see who was there?" asked Perlow.

"No, unfortunately, she didn't."

"This Isidore might have turned on the TV, and then slipped outside without anyone noticing."

"And then he met up with Dorothy somewhere," said Ronny.

"Oh no, I don't think they would have done that," Rubles objected. "Someone would have noticed that both the host and hostess were missing. Someone is always asking for a corkscrew or bottle opener at parties."

"*Eh bien,* Madame Rubles, I defer to your superior knowledge of dinner parties. That leaves us with two persons still unaccounted for, Madame Molly and Madame Edith."

"Three persons, Mr. P.," said Ronny. "We also need to account for Monsieur Irving."

Perlow admitted his mistake with a shrug.

They all turned to look at Miss Eppel.

"It's very possible Irving Miller also was watching TV. I believe Bernice said Molly had gone off to a corner in the dining room and was doing some yoga exercises, or meditations, or something like that."

From Miss Eppel's tone, it was

clear she did not approve of such things.

"As for Edith, Bernice said she didn't know where Edith had wandered off to."

There was a silence. Herschel Perlow took control of the conversation.

"We have, then, three suspects: Dorothy, who we know left the house, Edith Miller, who may have left, and Irving Miller, who also may have left the house."

"I suppose we should also add Isidore Miller to the list," said Rubles. "We don't really know if he was there or not, do we?"

"Now, Miss Eppel, did your friend Bernice mention if she or her husband had had a quarrel with any of these people? Could she think of any reason why one of them would play such a distasteful trick on her or her husband?"

"She was on quite good terms with them all. That is what made the whole thing so perplexing."

"What happened next?" asked Rubles. "That's my axiom. If at first you don't know where to go, go forward."

"And get coshed on the head," said Ronny.

"Only sometimes, dear. Now do let Miss Eppel get on with her story."

"Well, at some point in the evening Dorothy returned with a small plate of latkes, and everyone came back to the dining room, from wherever they'd been, and they finished the meal."

"No one looked, how do you say, with the ruffled feathers?" asked Perlow.

"I believe Bernice did say that Dorothy was looking rather frazzled for the rest of the evening. But one would expect that when a dinner party goes wrong."

"That's why Ronny and I never did anything formal," said Rubles. "Too much stress, for my taste."

"And the gentlemen?" asked Perlow.

"They seemed all right. Although Bernice did mention the party broke up early. Bernice and Max went straight home. And if you want to know if they went into the library before they retired for the night, the answer is no. They went upstairs and to bed."

"Order and method, Miss Eppel. What about the front door? When they returned home, was it locked or unlocked?"

"It was locked."

Perlow looked unhappy.

Agatha, who had been following the story as best she could, said, "I suppose someone at the dinner party might have had a key to their home, if they were old friends. My nephew Sheldon had a key to my home, in case I fell."

"That was very wise of you, dear," said Miss Eppel. "And very astute. Because this is, of course, how the person got in. They had a key to

Bernice's home, which they hadn't returned. When Bernice and Max had gone on holiday, they had given the friend the spare key so the friend could see to the mail and turn on lights. That sort of thing. And you know how busy one gets and forgets things. So the key was never returned."

"Well, who was it?" Rubles asked.

"And why did they put a dead dummy in the library?" asked Ronny.

"It was difficult to know how to proceed, because there didn't seem to be any motive," said Miss Eppel. "Even if it were just a childish prank, there usually is a darker reason for why the prank was done."

"This Max . . . Mannheim . . ."

"Mansfield, Mr. Perlow. Bernice and Max Mansfield."

"He was an accountant? Perhaps he was the accountant for the Millers' jewelry shop?"

"Oh no, nothing like that. He was a dentist."

"That's not helpful," said Ronny, "unless there was malpractice done."

"None of the Millers were his patients."

"Without a motive, there can be no crime," said Perlow, with disgust. "You have led us to the mare's nest, and we have fallen into it, fools that we are."

"Of course, this wasn't really a crime," said Rubles, following a line of her own. "I mean, it must have been unpleasant to discover the thing in one's home. But there was no real harm done, thank God."

"Yes, thank God for that," said Miss Eppel. "That's the point."

Miss Eppel allowed herself a small smile of satisfaction as she gazed at the astonished faces staring back at her. She then said, with a note of triumph, "The real crime was stopped before it could be committed."

"The real crime?" muttered Agatha. The story was beginning to sound vaguely familiar.

"I only realized it when Bernice and I returned to the library after our breakfast. The light outside had changed and there was now a strong beam of sunlight shining on the mannequin's face. I could see there was something on the thing's mouth, something shiny. It looked as though she had been eating something greasy and hadn't wiped her lips. That was ridiculous, I know, because a mannequin doesn't eat. But it did give me an idea."

Miss Eppel paused and waited.

"That's the clue?" asked Ronny.

"Yes, Mr. Bernfeld."

"What do you say, Rubles?"

"It might have been olive oil, from when the menorah tipped over, but you said it was a friend who put the dummy there and not Bernice or Max. So I suppose the grease might have come from some food, like chips or . . . of course, latkes. But why would anyone wipe a dummy's face with a latke? Do you know, Mr. Perlow?"

Rubles looked over at Herschel Perlow, who had leaned back in his chair, with his eyes closed.

"There is a pattern," he murmured. "I can see the pieces. All that is needed is to arrange them in the right way."

While Perlow arranged his pieces in his head, the others finished a rather watery cream of tomato soup.

"The car of Madame Dorothy, was it parked in the front of the house or the back?" asked Perlow, his eyes still closed.

"Their garage is in the back," replied Miss Eppel. She then said to the others, "I wonder if anyone wants that last piece of bread. Such a pity to let it get stale."

Ronny reached for the bread basket. To his surprise it was no longer on the table.

"That's the second clue, isn't it?" said Rubles. "You are a sly one, dear Miss Eppel."

Miss Eppel, who had hid the bread basket in her lap when no one was looking, put it back on the table. "There is so much in life we don't notice."

"*Eh bien,* Madame Dorothy puts the pan of latkes in her car when no one is looking. Later, she pretends it has disappeared."

"But why?" asked Rubles. "It only caused her trouble . . ." She stopped and stared at Miss Eppel. "There was something wrong with those latkes, wasn't there?"

"I'm afraid so, dear."

"Arsenic, I suppose," said Agatha. "Detective writers overuse it, but it does do the job, if you're an amateur."

"But how did Dorothy know the latkes were poisoned?" asked Rubles. "Wasn't it Bella and Sam who brought them?"

Perlow opened his eyes. Once again they had a queer gray light in them. "Brought, yes, but who made them? That is the question, as your Shakespeare says. Madame Bella? Not if she was sick with flu. Her husband Sam? A gambler may know how to stack the deck, but grating potatoes requires a different skill set entirely."

"You caught that? How very clever of you," Miss Eppel said.

"Not at all," said Perlow with a feigned air of modesty. "If brothers do not get along, why do they get together every Sunday night? It cannot be for the dinner, where they will bicker over trifles and get the indigestion. It therefore must be for the poker game that follows — a chance to earn some easy money, if the other players are not as skilled as you."

"There was some grumbling at the Sisterhood meetings," Miss Eppel agreed. "Edith, especially, complained that Sam cheated. That's only rumor, of course."

"So if Bella and Sam didn't make the latkes, who did?" asked Rubles. Then, answering her own question, "It must have been Dorothy. After Sam and Bella called to say they weren't coming for dinner, she must have seen her chance and cooked a batch of potato pancakes with arsenic and sent them over. That's why she put them in her car later, when the arsenic latkes got mixed up with the other ones. She knew they were dangerous and she didn't want anyone else to eat them. But why did she wish to poison Sam and Bella?"

"I suppose it was Sam who found out Isidore had cooked the books," said Ronny.

"Sam was always very clever with figures," Miss Eppel agreed. "It was a pity he didn't use his brains for something steady and legal, like being an accountant. Instead, when Irving said he wanted to retire and Isidore said they hadn't the money, Sam got suspicious. One night, he snuck into the shop after hours and looked over the books. He discovered that Isidore had been taking money out of the business for years. When he discovered the truth, he tried to blackmail Isidore."

"And Isidore thought a much better solution was to do away with Sam," said Perlow. "Yes, that would be very convenient. Isidore could do away with his blackmailer and pin the blame for the embezzlement on the deceased Sam at the same time. We are back in the Garden of Eden."

"But there was no dummy in Eden, Mr. P.," said Ronny. "You still haven't explained that."

Rubles had taken out a small notebook and pencil and she was writing down a list. "One, Bella and Sam cancel, because Bella has the flu. Two, Dorothy makes a nice batch of latkes laced with arsenic, to send to Bella and Sam. Three, Bella and Sam show up with the latkes — that must have given Dorothy a fright. Four, Dorothy puts the latkes in her car, to dispose of later. Five, when the others insist they want latkes, she drives to her sister's home and . . . And what? Asks her sister if she happens to have a dummy in the living room that she can spare?"

Rubles looked around at the others, to see if any of them cared to take up the thread of the story. Then she shook her head. "We do seem to stumble over that dummy every time."

"Actually," said Miss Eppel, "it was the dummy that told me everything."

"How so, Miss Eppel?" asked Ronny.

"Rubles actually came very close to my own thoughts. Most people don't have a mannequin lying around their home, unless they're a dressmaker, I suppose. So I had to think, who would? A jeweler's shop will often have a mannequin's head and upper torso on display some-where, to show off a necklace or two. But it's not impossible to have a full-length mannequin on hand. That seemed to me to be the most logical explanation for how the dummy was so quickly acquired. Someone must have known there was a mannequin in the Millers' jewelry shop, perhaps in storage."

Herschel Perlow nodded his ap-proval. "So Madame Dorothy first goes to her husband's shop and gets the mannequin. Then she drives to the home of Bernice and Max Mansfield and deposits the dummy in the library. We progress. But we are still lacking one thing: a motive. Only a crazy person would do such a thing."

Miss Eppel shook her head. "Dorothy Miller was not crazy. She was just very, very wicked. When I noticed the grease mark on the mannequin's lips, I knew exactly what she had done — and why. I therefore asked Bernice if we might remove the dummy's head. Bernice looked a little peculiar. 'You want to cut off her head?' she asked. 'Wouldn't that be rather violent, Janice?'

"I assured Bernice I wasn't going to chop off the thing's head. I just wanted to unscrew it so I could see if a little idea of mine was correct. So we unscrewed the head. I reached inside the body, and found what I was looking for."

"The missing money?" Rubles asked, rather breathlessly.

"No, dear. The latkes."

"Oh." Rubles looked disappointed.

"We asked that nice police detective to come back. He took the latkes to be tested. And my suspicions were correct. Arsenic had been added to the potato pancake batter. That's how we knew, you see, it was arsenic that had been added to the batter and not something else."

"I still don't understand why Dorothy didn't just dump the plate of latkes in some garbage pail," said Rubles. "Why the elaborate charade with the dummy, when she knew there was a good chance the latkes would be discovered?"

"It was actually very clever of her," replied Miss Eppel. "The dummy with the knife and the arsenic-flavored latkes caused quite a sensation in our little community, especially when the story made the front page of our local Jewish newspaper. Everyone was talking about it. But I think there was only one person who understood the meaning behind the incident — that it was a warning of some kind, as I had originally thought — and this person was Sam. If he continued with his threats to blackmail Isidore, he could expect another attempt on his life in return."

"I suppose Dorothy got a life sentence," said Agatha, who tried to be accurate in her mystery novels. "It was attempted murder."

Miss Eppel shook her head. "The case never came to court. You see, there was no real proof Dorothy Miller had done anything wrong. Anyone could have stuffed latkes down a mannequin's throat, dressed it up and gotten it into the Mansfields' library somehow, without being caught. Without fingerprints or some other way to conclusively tie the mannequin's poisoned latkes with the ones Dorothy had sent to Sam and Bella, there was nothing the police could do. She was very, very clever."

Agatha looked distressed. She didn't like it when criminals got off scotch free in books. If life was messy, she liked to think fiction was one place where justice could prevail. Then she remembered that this was real life.

"I suppose she didn't care about the embarrassment she caused the Mansfields," said Agatha.

"The Dorothy Millers of the world never do."

"But how did you know, Miss Eppel?" asked Ronny. "You said the story about Isidore Miller embezzling money only came out later."

"That's very true, Mr. Bernfeld. But, you see, I had been on the Sisterhood finance committee when Dorothy was its chairwoman. There was a problem with disappearing funds there as well. We could never prove who took the money, but I did have my suspicions.

"But she didn't get away with it," Miss Eppel added. "There is a God, you know, and He doesn't need fingerprints to determine if someone has attempted to murder someone else. Two months later, Dorothy and Isidore were driving on an icy road and skidded into a tree. They didn't survive, I'm afraid."

They were all silent for several moments. Death, even when deserved, was never a pleasant thing to encounter.

A waitress came to their table with the next course. "Here you are, ducks. We've got a nice surprise for you for your holiday. Piping hot potato pancakes to go with your fish. Eat them up while they're hot."

The waitress put the platters of fish and latkes on the table. The latkes were still sitting there when the waitress came back with the creamed spinach.

EVIL UNDER
THE WICK

Herschel Perlow was the first to shake off the air of solemnity that had fallen upon them all. Reaching for one of the latkes with his fork, he said, "We do not have to worry about the good Maggie trying to poison us. We are the geese that lay the golden eggs for Barnet Court. Without our monthly payments, the Maggies of the world would have no jobs."

"Applesauce or sour cream, Mr. Perlow?" asked Rubles.

"Sour cream, madame. I do not eat sweet things with my meal. It dulls the taste buds."

Rubles passed him the small bowl with the sour cream. Perlow took a generous helping and put it on the side of his plate. He then cut off a piece of latke, dipped it in the sour cream, and took a bite.

"I suppose one could hide arsenic in sour cream just as well as in whipped cream," said Rubles. "I remember reading about someone who did that. The maid put the arsenic in the topping of the trifle."

Mr. Perlow began to cough.

"Oh, dear," said Miss Eppel. "Did it go down the wrong way?"

"I believe one is supposed to put one's hands over one's head, when choking," said Agatha.

Mr. Perlow, still coughing and choking, took a sip of water instead. "Please, Madame Rubles," he said, after he had recovered, "may we not speak any more about poisons."

"I'm so sorry. I suppose there is a time and place for everything."

"That reminds me of something," said Ronny. "I wish I could remember what."

Herschel Perlow replaced his glass on the table. "Memory, it is an interesting topic that."

"Some people don't like it that when you are older you can't remember what you've done in the morning, yet you can remember perfectly what happened during your first visit to the sea," said Miss

Eppel. "I personally find the old memories comforting. One doesn't feel so very alone."

"That is because your old memories are comforting," replied Perlow. "But I was not speaking of this kind of memory, the memories of the elderly. I was thinking of a memory that helped me solve a very interesting crime."

Perlow took another bite of latke.

"You are going to tell us the story, Mr. Perlow?" said Rubles.

Perlow waved his fork, as he said, "A thousand pardons, Madame Rubles, but I have not the talents of the raconteur."

Rubles and Ronny exchanged glances. They knew that when Herschel Perlow assumed a mantle of false modesty there was nothing to do but to coax him with flattery.

"You can't fool us, Monsieur Perlow," said Ronny. "You could have written the book when it comes to solving mysteries. Isn't that so, Miss Eppel?"

Miss Eppel looked flustered. "Well, I am certain Mrs. Krinsky must also be very good at writing books."

"Oh, of course," said Rubles. "Ronny didn't mean to imply otherwise."

"All friends here," Ronny assured the new addition to their table. "But some of us happen to know our friend Mr. P. can tell a rousing tale, when he wants."

Perlow glanced over at Agatha.

"With your permission, madame?"

It was Agatha's turn to look flustered. "I would very much like to hear Monsieur Perlow's story, but about the body I found this morning. Perhaps we could discuss it first."

"Order and method, Mrs. Krinsky," said Ronny. "Isn't that right, Perlow?"

Perlow bowed in Ronny Bernfeld's direction. He then patted down his hair. It bounced back. "*Mes amis,* I agree to tell my story on one condition. I will tell what happened, without interruptions. At the end, you will each have a turn to say what, in your opinion, is the correct solution. Are we agreed?"

The longtime residents of Barnet Court assured Perlow of their assent. Agatha once again retreated into silence. She was beginning to feel slightly off balance, a feeling she had had too often after this last fall. It was absurd, of course, but she couldn't shake the feeling she had met all these people somewhere before. In the meantime, Perlow had begun to speak. Perhaps something in his story would jar something in her memory and she would remember.

"My story, too, took place many years ago," he said. "It was a time when there was still such a thing as glamor in the world. There was a place for chivalry as well. But, alas, even then they were disappearing.

101

They were being replaced by the rock and roll."

The others made suitably disapproving sounds.

"I was vacationing at a seaside resort in Wales. Its name was The Mumbles, if I recall correctly — a peculiar name, but there are so many peculiar names in your amiable country. My hotel was a small one and secluded. The clientele were the rich and the very rich."

"You could afford such a place, so soon after the war?" asked Rubles.

Perlow glared.

"Oops! Sorry, Monsieur Perlow. I forgot. I'll be quiet."

"As I was saying, there were only a select few guests and twice as many staff to dance attendance upon us. There was a young couple who had been married perhaps four or five years, a Mr. and Mrs. White. In contrast, a middle-aged American couple, Mr. and Mrs. Hapstein, had been married thirty years or so, I would say. There was also a young author, a Mr. Howard Blum. And, last but not least, there was the financier Mr. Arnold Glick, his twelve-year-old daughter Louise, and his second wife, Irene."

"Those last names sound familiar," said Agatha. "Hadn't Irene been a model or on the stage, before she married Arnold Glick?"

"Please, Madame Agatha, all in good time." Perlow brought his hands together and gently tapped the tips of his fingers against one another, while he re-boarded his train of thought. "There also was the proprietress of the hotel, a widow, whose name was Mrs. Winters. By some coincidence, all of us had arrived at the hotel on the same day, which kept Mrs. Winters very busy. That evening, when the cocktails were served, the introductions were made and the small talk was spoken. By the time we were shown into the dining room, it was clear a miserable time was in the offing. This was not only due to the chilling effect on the spirits of an English resort in the wintertime, when the sky is gray and the scene is desolate. There are those who enjoy the bracing winds and the dramatic seascapes."

Mr. Perlow arranged his woolen scarf more tightly around his neck.

"Alas, Mr. and Mrs. White were in a black mood," he continued. "Nothing pleased the young woman, despite her husband's efforts to find her the comfortable seat, because Madame did not like to sit in the draft; to find her the orangeade, because Madame did not drink alcohol; to find her the carrot and celery sticks, because Madame did not eat the prepared hors d'oeuvres. Me, I was worn out from watching Monsieur White run after the waiters, in an attempt to please his wife.

"As for Mr. and Mrs. Hapstein, the American couple, there was nothing that did not please the middle-aged woman. She adored the great hearth in the sitting room, even though the fire was sending billows of smoke into the room. She thought the half-timbered ceiling was too quaint for words, although she must have uttered two dozen of them to say so. She praised the hors d'oeuvres for being exactly like her friends back in Omaha had told her they would be: soggy and without taste. Try as I might to escape, her booming voice filled the room, which made me wonder if her husband was slightly deaf or wore the ear stoppers."

"Plugs," said Rubles. "I'm not interrupting, but the correct term is ear plugs."

"*Eh bien,* the ear plugs. When I saw the young author sitting in a corner by himself, I went over to make the polite conversation. I asked what his book was about.

" 'Nothing,' he replied.

" 'It is a book of philosophy? You ask the eternal questions?'

"He gave the look, the look that was meant to make me feel like nothing. Fortunately, I have the thick skin. So I asked, 'You are a physicist then?'

" 'I am neither philosopher nor scientist,' he replied. 'I write novels.'

" 'But a novel must be about something,' I said.

" 'My novel does not.'

"At that moment the summons

came to enter the dining room. Mr. Blum and I parted company and each went our own way to our places at the table."

Rubles was about to ask a question, but she caught herself in time. Perlow, however, had noticed.

"You are correct, Madame Rubles. Where were the exceptionally rich Mr. Glick, his daughter Louise, and his beautiful wife Irene? While the rest of us were in the large sitting room where the cocktails were being served, Mr. Glick and his daughter were seated in a small alcove, playing checkers. As he explained later, it was not to be rude or stand-offish. But he saw his daughter so little — his business affairs kept him very busy —

that he wished to spend as much time with Louise as possible during their holiday. As for Madame Irene, she made her grand entrance after the rest of us were already seated at table.

" 'I'm so sorry I'm late,' she said, not looking a bit sorry.

"She was very elegantly dressed in a reddish-brown brocade gown that went down to the floor. A velvet cape of the same color was draped over her shoulders. The color suited perfectly her pale complexion and jet black hair. The total effect was très chic. Yes, that one had the glamor."

"No jewels?" asked Ronny.

"I was coming to that, Monsieur Bernfeld."

"Sorry, Mr. P."

"All of the ladies were wearing jewels. Mrs. White wore a simple strand of pearls. Mrs. Hapstein wore some sort of gold monstrosity about her neck."

"Which probably cost a small fortune," said Rubles.

Perlow ignored the comment. "Mrs. Glick wore a necklace of diamonds. The larger stones were perhaps five carats, each one of perfect cut and clarity. Only *la petite* Louise was without the jewels.

"After dinner, we returned to the sitting room. Coffee was served. There was a grand piano in the room, and Mr. White sat down and began to play. He was very good. He played the popular songs. Mrs.

Hapstein seemed to be enjoying the music, although she announced to the world she could not carry a tune. I thanked *le bon Dieu* she did not try to sing along. Mr. Hapstein also looked thankful. He was not one that one noticed much, but he seemed to be the good sport. He applauded at the end of each song, laughed when someone said a joke. My little idea, at the time, was that it was Mrs. Hapstein who was possessed of the great fortune. Mr. Hapstein did not have the air of one to the manor born, as you English like to say.

"But then the poor Mrs. White complained the music was giving her a headache, and why did Mr. White insist on playing the piano when he knew it gave her a headache, and why did he not have her little pills with him when he knew she was always tired after traveling and . . . You understand how it was between them. Mrs. White left the salon and went to her room. Mr. White gave us all a hurried goodnight, and he followed her.

"Mrs. Hapstein wished to play bridge, but everyone declined. Mr. Glick decided it was time for Louise to go to bed, and the Glick family left the room. I was not in the mood for cards and so I made my excuses, claiming I was too tired after my travels to concentrate on the game. Mr. Blum had disappeared to somewhere after dinner.

"The room began to clear out, until I was the last guest. I had only feigned tiredness, you understand. I was actually wide awake and restless. There was something in the air, a feeling something was about to happen. It is what you English call 'the atmosphere.' I wished to think, to arrange my impressions of the day — and the guests.

"But not long after I had arranged myself in a comfortable chair before the fire, which was no longer sending smoke into the room, Mrs. Winters entered. When she saw me, she sat in the chair beside me.

" 'I like to sit in this room for a few minutes at the end of the day,' she explained.

" 'It is hard work, running a small

hotel,' I said.

" 'I can't complain.'

"We were silent for several minutes. Then she said, 'I do wish I could do something for the Whites, something to cheer that woman up. They are too young to be so unhappy.'

" 'It is not always easy to be young. The author, Mr. Blum, he is not happy either.'

" 'He'll get over it. I get a fair amount of young authors and painters as guests, at least the ones with parents willing to pay for their whims. They have to pretend to be miserable, otherwise their work doesn't sell. Once they realize they haven't any talent, they're usually much happier.'

"We talked for a few more minutes. Then Mrs. Winters said she had to make sure everything was locked up for the night. I closed my eyes for a moment. The chair was very comfortable. Perhaps I dozed. I only recall opening my eyes with a start. Someone was creeping down the staircase, someone who did not know a certain step creaked loudly in the silent night. I jumped from my chair, but I had the presence of mind not to rush into the hall. Instead, I stood by the doorway to the sitting room, where I could hear without being seen.

" 'Mrs. Winters?' I heard a young female's voice call out. It was Mademoiselle Louise.

"I went into the hall and explained that Mrs. Winters was most likely busy at the back of the house. 'But I am at your service, mademoiselle,' I said, bowing as I said so. 'Perhaps I can assist you.'

" 'The light in my lamp has burned out,' she said. 'I like to read before I go to sleep.'

"Mrs. Winters appeared in the hallway. She had heard Louise call. She went to fetch a new lightbulb. I thought *la petite* Louise would return to her room at once and await the light there. Instead, she stared at me. She had a most penetrating gaze for one so young.

" 'You're not really French, are you?' she said at last.

" 'No, mademoiselle, I am from Galicia.'

" 'That's Poland, isn't it?'

" 'The town I am from was in Ukraine. At least it was when I left it. The borders in that part of the world change almost as quickly as the seasons.'

"I laughed at my little joke. Louise did not.

" 'If you're not from France, why do you drop French words into your conversation?'

" 'You find it pretentious?'

" 'I find it stupid. I think it's stupid when people pretend to be something they're not.'

" 'Sometimes people have no choice,' I said.

" 'Why not?'

" 'You are young, Mademoi . . . I mean, Miss Louise.'

" 'That's what adults always say when they don't know what to answer.'

" 'You think I have no answer for you?'

" 'Yes, that's exactly what I think. Why do you have to pretend to be something you're not?'

" 'Perhaps today, I do not have to. But . . .'

"I noticed the girl was shivering. The hallway was not heated. I suggested we go to the sitting room and sit by the fire, until Mrs. Winters returned. When we were settled, Louise insisted I continue with my explanation. She had a strong will, that one. I hope she has used it for the good.

" 'I was a young man when the

Second World War broke out,' I told her. 'I lived with my family in a small town in Ukraine. My entire family was killed. My friends from school were killed, too. I am only alive because I fled to the forest and the good God watched over me. After the war I managed to smuggle myself into the West. I decided that if the world had no use for Herschel Perlowitz from Galicia, if no one cared if this Jew lived or died, perhaps I would do better as someone else. And so when I came to this country I became Herschel Perlow. I exchanged my poor English sprinkled with Yiddish for poor English sprinkled with the little French I had picked up along the way, and *voilà*! Here I am.'

"We could hear footsteps coming down the hall. At that hour, one could hear every sound. Mrs. Winters returned with a package of lightbulbs. She seemed surprised to see the two of us talking. Louise rose from her chair at once and went over to Mrs. Winters. The two climbed the stairs together. When they were halfway up, Louise turned and said to me, 'I'm sorry for what happened to you and your family. But I still think it's stupid to pretend to be something you're not.'

"Although I had gone to bed in a somber mood, I awoke to a pleasant surprise. The sun was shining, and it looked to be a glorious day. It was my habit to dine lightly at breakfast, but since I thought to take a walk and enjoy the sunny weather I filled my plate with scrambled eggs and potatoes and toast.

"It seemed everyone was in a better mood, after having had a good night's sleep. Even Madame White managed to smile at a little joke Mr. White made; about what, I do not recall.

"Mr. Blum was the first to rise from the table. 'I am going to the lighthouse today,' he said. He then turned to Mr. and Mrs. White. 'Would you care to join me? We can easily fit three in the boat.'

"Mr. White looked at his wife.

Everyone could see he was yearning to accept the invitation. Who knew if the good weather would last?

"But Mrs. White became angry. 'You know I get seasick, Alan.'

" 'Would you mind, Evelyn, if I went with Mr. Blum? He really shouldn't row out there alone.'

" 'And what am I supposed to do while you're gone?'

" 'Louise, didn't you say you wanted to do some sketching, while we were here?' said Mr. Glick. 'Why don't you and Mrs. White go down to the bay?'

"Louise glared at her father. As I believe I have already mentioned, she had a force, that little one.

" 'There's no reason why everyone's day has to be ruined,' said Mrs. White. 'I shall take a walk. Alone.' She then left the dining room in a puff."

"A huff, Mr. P.," said Ronny. "The expression would be she left the room in a huff."

Perlow raised his hands, as if to say to heaven, "These English and their absurd language." What he actually said was, "I continue, if there are no objections."

There were not.

"Mr. Blum looked discomfited. 'Sorry, old man,' he said.

" 'It's not your fault,' Mr. White assured him. 'And I do need to get out from time to time, otherwise I'll explode.'

" 'Mr. and Mrs. Hapstein, would

you like to come with us?' asked Mr. Blum. 'Your rowboats can hold four, can't they, Mrs. Winters?'

"Mrs. Winters assured them the boats were quite sound, but the American couple begged off.

" 'I'm not much of a sailor, I'm afraid,' said Mr. Hapstein.

" 'I need to write some letters,' said Mrs. Hapstein. 'If I don't, the folks back home will send for Scotland Yard, wondering where we are.'

"She laughed heartily at her joke, not caring if others laughed with her. She was the typical rich American lady, secure in the knowledge that with her bank account filled with dollars she owned the world.

"The young men asked if I would like to go with them, to be polite. I also made my apologies. I, too, suffer from the seasickness, although I do not like to broadcast my weaknesses. Mr. Blum and Mr. White went with Mrs. Winters to get a picnic lunch. Mrs. Hapstein retired to a small sitting room where there was a writing desk and stationery. I asked Mr. Hapstein if he would like to join me in a walk.

" 'Thank you, but no,' he said. 'I plan to grab a book, for show. But my real plan is to find a comfortable chair in the sun and take a nap. I never did see the point of running around and wearing yourself out when you're on vacation.'

"As for Mr. and Mrs. Glick and Louise, they had decided to rent a motor car and go exploring. They also took along a picnic lunch, I believe. And so the day marched on, each to his own drummer.

"I returned from my walk in time for lunch, and after the morning's exercise I had the good appetite. The food there was excellent, I might add, except for the hors d'oeuvres. Afterward, I decided to do as Mr. Hapstein had done in the morning. I sat on the veranda and closed my eyes.

"When I awoke, I saw that the day had grown gray and chilly. I was just about to go inside, when I heard a man shouting."

"The decisive moment, eh, Mr. P.?" said Ronny.

"As you say, Mr. Bernfeld, at last we arrive at the decisive moment."

Miss Eppel, who had felt her own eyes closing at the mention of a nap, jerked them wide open.

"It was Mr. White," Perlow continued. "He was running toward the hotel as if his life depended upon his reaching it in time. 'It's Howard! Mr. Blum! He's gone under! We've got to do something!'

"All at once there was a commotion. People came running from all corners of the hotel, guests as well as staff. Me, I thought to myself there was probably nothing to be done. If the poor young man had truly been lost to the sea, by this time he would have drowned. Still, we must make an effort. Even if there is only one chance in ten thousand of a happy end, we must do what we can to save a life. I could tell by Mrs. Winter's face she felt as I did, that our efforts would be for naught. But she, too, roused herself and gave orders to her staff.

"We all made our way to the sea. I was sorry I had not first gone for my winter coat, because the wind was strong and the icy sprays of water from the waves stung. While I and the other guests gazed out at the waves furiously crashing against the rocks, Mrs. Winters was in deep conversation with some of the young men of her staff.

" 'Why didn't you come back sooner?' Mr. Glick asked Mr. White. He was irritated, I could tell. 'Didn't you notice the weather was changing?'

" 'We did,' replied Mr. White. 'But Mr. Blum decided he wanted to go out again. He said he had handled boats since he was a child. He said this was his favorite weather to go out, when it was him against the sea.'

"Mrs. Winter came over to us. 'I can't send my boys out there. The sea is too rough. It would be suicidal to try to find Mr. Blum in this weather. I'm sorry. I'm so sorry.'

"She hurried away. I think she did not want us to see her cry. The members of her staff began to drift away as well.

" 'Father, can't we try to save him?' asked Louise.

"Mr. Glick shook his head. 'He was a fool to go out in this weather.

We would be bigger fools to follow him.'

"Irene Glick tried to put her arm around Louise. It was a pretty gesture, but Louise shook off Madame Glick's arm and began to run toward the hotel.

" 'It's tough for a kid,' said Mrs. Hapstein. 'I suppose this is her first encounter with death.'

" 'Yes, I think it is,' said Mr. Glick.

" 'We may as well go back to the hotel,' said Mrs. Hapstein to her husband.

"To compensate for the rebuff of his daughter, Mr. Glick put his arm around his wife and they also slowly walked away.

"Only I remained with Mr. White.

His eyes were still scanning the waves, hoping to catch a glimpse of the young author. At last, even he gave up.

" 'I shouldn't have let him go out again. I should have stopped him,' he said as we walked back to the hotel.

" 'Mr. Blum was a grown man. Perhaps it is true he had a wish for the suicide.'

" 'Why? He had his whole life ahead of him.'

"I thought back to our conversation the first night, and Mr. Blum's book about nothing. A person can live with very little, I thought. That I knew from my own experiences during the war. But nothing? No one can live without at least a shred of hope for a happier future.

Herschel Perlow took a sip from his water glass. During the pause, Agatha looked around at the others. They all looked so old. She supposed she looked old in their eyes, too. But they were still alive. Not just physically alive. Alive to life. She could see it in their eyes. Their hopes for the future might not be the same as those of a young person just out of school, but they still had them. She did, too. She had another book or two in her. She wanted to dance at the weddings of Sheldon and Jean's children. She wanted . . . But Perlow was continuing with his story.

"By the time we returned, the

hotel was in a different kind of flurry," he said. "In all the excitement about trying to find Mr. Blum, we had forgotten Chanukah was starting that night. But Mrs. Winters had not, and she was then instructing a few members of her staff to set up menorahs in the sitting room, for those who wished to light the first candle.

" 'I had planned a little party afterward,' she said, 'the dreidel game, songs, that sort of thing. But under the circumstances . . .'

" 'We'll just light and sing the traditional songs quietly,' said Mr. Glick.

"Despite our depressed spirits, the menorahs with their pretty colored candles lifted us up. There was no need to wait for everyone to arrive, because each family had its own menorah, so we could all fulfill the commandment. After I was shown to the place where my menorah was waiting, I said the blessings and lit the first candle. I had only just finished when I noticed that Mr. and Mrs. Hapstein were having some sort of argument with Mrs. Winters.

" 'I'm very sorry, but you cannot light a menorah in your room,' Mrs. Winters was saying. 'I don't allow it. It's a fire hazard.'

" 'And I don't allow your staff to move our things about the hotel," replied Mrs. Hapstein.

"I think we were all surprised by the American woman's angry outburst, although we were all perhaps more emotional than usual.

" 'They were only trying to be helpful, I'm sure.'

" 'My menorah is an antique," explained Mr. Hapstein, in his quiet way. 'It belonged to my grandfather.'

" 'And we don't intend to leave it sitting here in the lobby, where anyone can steal it,' said Mrs. Hapstein.

"While they were arguing with Mrs. Winters, I drifted over to the table where Mr. Hapstein's menorah had been placed. I assumed it was his, because it was the only one that was different than the others. It was a small travel menorah, made from silver. I noticed the holders were too small to fit a candle inside. Someone had therefore set beside the menorah a bottle of olive oil and a few wicks made from rolled cotton.

"Mrs. Hapstein must have seen me from the corner of her eye, because she suddenly turned and yelled, 'What do you think you're doing? Get away from our menorah!'

"She might have continued to yell, if we had not been interrupted by a piercing cry that made our blood freeze.

" 'It's Irene!' said Mr. Glick. He ran out of the room and up the stairs, where he was met by Mrs. Glick, whose face was deathly pale.

" 'My diamond necklace — it's

gone!'

"In that first moment, I believe Mr. Glick was grateful nothing worse had happened. Then the practical side of him took over. Mrs. Winters also had moved toward the stairs. Her face was showing the strain from the day's events.

" 'Shall I help you look for your necklace, Mrs. Glick?' she asked. 'Perhaps it's just been moved to a different place.'

" 'Thank you,' said Mr. Glick. 'That will be a help.'

"Mrs. Winters and Mrs. Glick went back upstairs. Mr. Glick returned to the sitting room.

" 'I say we leave this place tomorrow,' Mrs. Hapstein said to her husband. 'I felt there was something fishy the moment I heard the name. The Mumbles. What kind of name is that for an exclusive resort?'

" 'I suppose we should light the candles,' Mr. White said to his wife, who had been reading a book in the corner of the room. She listlessly set the book aside and followed her husband to their menorah.

" 'We'll wait until Mrs. Glick comes down,' Mr. Glick said to no one in particular. He guided his daughter to a settee and the two sat down.

" 'I was curious as to what Mr. Hapstein would decide to do. I could understand his not wanting to leave a valuable antique in an open room, but his menorah was small and it could not hold much oil, probably just enough to burn for half an hour — the amount of time to fulfill the mitzvah. I was going to suggest he wait in the sitting room while the light burned. Then he could return his menorah to his room. Apparently, he had had the same thought, because he had picked up the bottle of olive oil and was looking at it.

"Mrs. Winters and Mrs. Glick returned to the sitting room. From their faces it was obvious their search had not been met with success. The diamond necklace was still missing. Most likely, it had been stolen.

" 'I know what you are all thinking,' said Mrs. Winters, 'but the necklace wasn't taken by one of my staff. I am sure of it.'

" 'How can you be so sure?' asked Mr. Glick, who was trying very hard to remain civil.

" 'I pay them well, for one thing. For another, they're used to our guests arriving with their jewels. Such a thing has never happened here before.'

" 'Perhaps you have hired someone new?' I offered.

" 'No, I have not. They have all been with me for years.'

" 'If it wasn't one of your staff who took my wife's necklace, who did take it?' asked Mr. Glick.

"Mrs. Winters looked distressed.

" 'She thinks one of us took it, Daddy,' said *la petite* Louise.

" 'That's ridiculous,' said Mrs. White. She then turned to her husband and said, 'Are you going to allow this woman to insult us?'

"Mr. White was looking very tired, but he made the effort to calm down his wife. 'She can't suspect us, darling. Isn't that right, Mrs. Winters?'

"There was a silence. I stepped forward and said, 'Madame Winters, I insist you search my room.'

" 'I . . . It's very good of you, Monsieur Perlow, but I'd rather not have to do that. It is possible someone took the necklace by mistake and . . .'

" 'By mistake? That's the most ridiculous thing I've ever heard,' said Mr. Glick. 'If Mrs. Winters won't search your room, Mr. Perlow, have you any objections to my doing it for her?'

" 'None at all,' I said.

" 'I say we all go together and search our rooms,' suggested Mrs. Hapstein. 'No one minds if my husband stays here with his menorah, do you? I don't like the way things are starting to disappear.'

"Mr. Glick assured her that he had no objections.

" 'You can light without me,' Mrs. Hapstein called out to her husband, as we went to the stairs.

"The search of our rooms was unsuccessful," Perlow said to the others. "We returned to the sitting room — and I arrived at the solution to the puzzle. There, I have talked enough. Now it is your turn to offer a solution. Who stole the necklace?"

Perlow looked around the table. "Mr. Bernfeld, perhaps you would like to begin?"

Ronny shifted in his chair uneasily. "I always believe in ladies first."

"Madame Rubles?"

"The first person to speak is always at such a disadvantage," she said. "Are we allowed to ask questions now, Monsieur Perlow?"

"You may ask. If I can answer, I will."

"Very well, then. Would you say that Mr. and Mrs. Glick were happily married?"

Perlow considered. "You understand, I had known them for less than forty-eight hours when the theft occurred. But, yes, I would say they were reasonably happy."

Rubles looked unhappy. "Even so, I still think it was Mrs. Glick who stole her own necklace. She very likely needed money and intended to sell it when she got back to London — and collect the insurance money.'

"You're wrong, Rubles," said Ronny. "It had to be the Whites. All that arguing — way overdone, in my opinion. And don't forget Mrs. White had all morning to sneak into Mrs. Glick's room and take the necklace, while the Glicks were out motoring."

"If she took it, where did she hide

it?" asked Rubles. "They searched everyone's rooms."

"You missed the clue Mr. P. snuck in when they were back in the sitting room. Mrs. White was sitting on a chair, reading a book. She probably knew a search would be made of the bedrooms, so she hid the necklace under the chair cushion. She'd retrieve it later."

Ronny sat back in his chair, feeling very smug.

Perlow turned to Miss Eppel. "Do you agree with Mr. or Mrs. Bernfeld, or have you an idea of your own?"

Miss Eppel's cheeks turned pink. "I'm sure they are both much cleverer than I am. But I do feel, in this instance at least, they are on the wrong track."

"The crime reminds you of something that happened at a Sisterhood meeting?" asked Ronny, with a smile.

"You laugh, Mr. Bernfeld, but it does. Of course, what was taken wasn't nearly as valuable as a diamond necklace. But it was quite awkward for Mrs. Levy when she discovered her stepdaughter had stolen her house keys out of her purse. Lillian, that was the name of the girl, had snuck into the room where we were having our meeting, while we took a break for tea. She thought if she threw away her stepmother's keys, Mrs. Levy would never be able to get in their home again. Lillian was just a young child, much younger than the Louise of your story, Monsieur Perlow. But the relationship between a second wife and her stepdaughter is never easy."

"You cast your vote, then, for Mademoiselle Louise?" asked Perlow.

"Yes, I think she took the necklace, out of spite."

"When did she have the opportunity?" asked Ronny.

Miss Eppel looked flustered. "I can't say exactly. But she would only need a minute or two. Perhaps she came down to breakfast a few minutes later than her parents."

"And where did she hide it?" demanded Rubles.

"Oh, girls are very good at hiding things," said Miss Eppel. "She probably stuffed it into a stocking or a coat pocket. I don't imagine they did such a thorough search of her room. It would not have been nice for Mr. Glick to feel his daughter was under suspicion."

"Well, Mr. Perlow?" asked Rubles. "Who is right?"

"Wait, we haven't asked Mrs. Krinsky for her opinion," said Ronny.

"Sorry, you've been so quiet I almost forgot you were here," said Rubles.

Agatha wished her mind felt clearer. It was so disconcerting to feel like a solution was just within reach, but she couldn't grasp it. "I am inclined to agree with Mr. Bernfeld, although I can't say exactly why," she said.

"That's all right, Mrs. Krinsky," said Ronny. "All that matters is that you're on the winning team. Isn't that so, Mr. P.?"

"No, Monsieur B., you are not the winning team," said Perlow. "None of you are. The person who stole the necklace was Howard Blum."

"Impossible!" exclaimed Rubles. "He died."

"He was out all day in the boat, with Mr. White," said Ronny. "If it was Blum who stole the necklace, the Whites had to be in on it, too."

"Let me explain how I arrived at the solution, with method and order," said Perlow, hushing the others. "As you recall, I said earlier

I arrived at the solution when we returned to the sitting room, after we had made a search of our rooms. What exactly did I see, you may ask?"

"All right, we're asking," said Ronny. "What did you see?"

"I saw Mr. Hapstein still standing by his menorah, which was not yet lit."

"Why didn't he light it?" asked Rubles.

"Because he could not." Herschel Perlow's eyes were shining with an odd light.

"We'll play the game," said Ronny. "Why couldn't he light it?"

"I mentioned the holders were too small to hold candles, so the staff had brought him a bottle of olive oil and a few wicks made from rolled cotton. I saw the bottle was no longer full, which suggested Mr. Hapstein had poured some oil into the holder for the first light. Yet he was still holding one of the wicks in his hand, as though he didn't know what to do with it."

"If it was his menorah, why wouldn't he know what to do with the wick?"

"Precisely, Madame Rubles. Granted, on the first night of Chanukah one forgets certain things, perhaps the exact wording of all three blessings. But a person does not forget how to light his own menorah. He does not forget that when using a cotton wick and oil, one needs something to hold the wick upright.

"I had seen these small menorahs before. Not exactly like the one Mr. Hapstein had, you understand, but something similar. I therefore knew there usually was a small drawer in the base of the menorah to hold a supply of wicks and the little metal holders to keep the wick upright. Why, then, had not Mr. Hapstein opened the little drawer?"

Rubles began to smile. "I don't suppose you decided to help him out?"

Monsieur Perlow shrugged. "What could I do? I see a man in obvious distress. I believe I have a solution. So I took the menorah from Mr. Hapstein's hands. I opened the little drawer. I removed the thin metal holders. And there, sitting under the supply of cotton wicks, was . . ."

Rubles completed the sentence. "The latkes!"

Ronny and Rubles burst into laughter, while Miss Eppel hid a smile behind the blanket she was crocheting. Perlow, glaring at them with disfavor, smoothed down his hair. It bounced back up.

"Sorry, Mr. P., but I couldn't resist," said Rubles. "It was the necklace, wasn't it?"

"Yes, madame, the necklace was inside the drawer."

Miss Eppel shook her head with disapproval. "Such wickedness. A menorah is a holy object. It shouldn't have been used for an evil purpose."

"I agree, with all my heart," said Perlow.

"Why didn't Mr. Hapstein remove the necklace and hide it when the others went upstairs?" asked Rubles.

"Why, indeed? Unfortunately, Mr. Hapstein was not the brains of the operation. When someone told him what to do, he did it. But he was one of those people who can't think on their own."

"But where does Howard Blum come in?" asked Ronny.

"You, Monsieur Bernfeld, were on the right track when you said the Whites' arguing seemed overdone. But it seems Madame Evelyn White truly was a very unhappy person. Because she was also a very rich woman, her husband, who had no fortune of his own, put up with her moods.

"However, there was another guest at the hotel whose behavior was also exaggerated — our American friend, Mrs. Hapstein. Even before the theft, I suspected there was something not on the level about her and her husband. But it was only when I saw Mr. Hapstein from the profile, when he was standing with the wick in his hands, that I saw the resemblance between him and his son."

"His son?" asked Agatha, genuinely perplexed. This was not at all like the solution she had been working out in her mind.

"Yes, Madame Krinsky. Howard Blum, or Howard Hapstein or whatever name he will use the next time, was the son of the American couple. Of course, they are not really Americans. They are as British as you or me. But they have a talent for the accents, and the disguise."

"But Howard Blum drowned," said Ronny. "Mr. White saw him go under."

"No, *mon ami.* Monsieur White saw him go under the water. Monsieur White saw the boat drift without Monsieur Blum in it. He did not see a body return to shore."

"You mean, Mr. Blum just pretended to go under?" said Rubles. "But he was really hiding somewhere near the shore?"

"That is what jogged my memory," said Perlow. "I had heard about a similar case where a young man tragically drowned, and a theft was discovered at a nearby hotel not long after. And so I wondered. Yes, I wondered if this was a co-incidence or was the match striking a second time."

"I think you mean lightning, Mr. Perlow," said Rubles. "It's lightning that isn't supposed to strike a second time, although I think that's just a myth."

Perlow acknowledged his mistake with a shrug. "While everyone was rushing to the shore, Mr. Blum took a different path to return to the hotel by the back entrance. He ran into Mrs. Glick's room, took the necklace, ran to his parents' room and stuck the necklace inside the drawer at the base of his father's menorah, as the three of them had planned earlier. It was an excellent idea, because the drawer is not apparent to someone who is not familiar with these travel menorahs. One has to look closely to see it. But he had not counted on Herschel Perlow being among the guests. Nor had he anticipated that someone would move the menorah down to the sitting room."

"What did he do after he hid the necklace?" asked Rubles. "Wasn't it dangerous to remain in the hotel?"

"It was. That is why after he hid the necklace, he slipped out of the hotel and found a hiding place, where he intended to remain until it was dark. Then he would make his escape to another town, where he would wait for his parents to join him."

"Did they ever find the boy?" asked Miss Eppel.

"You are wondering if he was sent to jail or if he slipped through the fingers of the police?"

"Yes, I am."

"They found him, and I do not think he will try such a stunt in winter ever again. He had caught a bad cold, hiding outside in the wet clothes. When I searched the rocks and caves with the police, we had only to follow the sound of the sneezes."

"I hope he didn't get pneumonia," said Miss Eppel.

"No," said Monsieur Perlow. "He got seven years."

AND THEN THERE WERE *GORNISHT*

The waitress had taken away their plates. While they waited for dessert to be served, Agatha once again tried to turn the conversation round to the body she had found in the library before lunch. It was one thing for a younger woman like the arts and crafts instructor to not take her seriously; the young had a distressing tendency to think that "old" was a synonym for "foolish." But she could not understand why her luncheon companions refused to believe she really had found a dead body.

Perhaps this was payback time, she thought. For fifty years she had made a living from deceiving people, planting red herrings in her books so people would think the wrong person was the murderer. Now, no one would believe her when she did speak the truth.

But this wasn't the first time in her life she had encountered an obstacle. There had been a few occasions when her publishers were lukewarm about a manuscript, suggesting that perhaps the creative well had run dry. When that happened, she had gone back to her typewriter with even greater resolve, determined to make the next book her best. And the new book often surprised her, as well as her readers and the critics.

She therefore decided the problem must be that she hadn't presented her discovery of the body in a sufficiently exciting way. The modern world was so noisy and filled with so many distractions. Perhaps a person could no longer say, "There's a dead body in the library. We'd better call the police." Perhaps you had to take a photo of the body on your cell phone and send it to Facebook and Instagram and WhatsApp and those other names Sheldon was always mentioning. Then, when your post went viral — the word "viral" always made her think of some dreaded disease gone wild, like the influenza epidemic of 1918 — perhaps the right people would take notice.

Unfortunately, she didn't know where her phone was at the moment. She supposed Sheldon had remembered to pack it with her other things this morning, when she left the rehab facility. Perhaps it was in her tote bag, with her medication. When she returned to her room, she must look for it. If no one else was willing to call the police, she must do it herself. She only hoped the battery wasn't dead. She very often forgot to recharge it. But surely there was a regular phone in her room. She could use that if . . .

"Have you ever been there, Mrs.

Krinsky?"

Agatha returned to the other world, the world that wasn't inside her head, with a start. "I'm sorry, Mr. Bernfeld, I'm afraid I wasn't paying attention. I was thinking about the body I found in the library. The one I told you about."

"Oh, well, if you want to tell your story before we tell ours, I'm sure Rubles and I won't object. I only thought that because our story also takes place near the sea — one of the uninhabited Isles of Scilly, to be precise — it made sense to carry on with the seafaring theme."

"These names!" exclaimed Herschel Perlow. "First The Mumbles, now the Silly Islands. Why are they called silly? Do people act foolishly there all the time?"

"Not S-i-l-l-y, Mr. P.," said Ronny. "It's spelled S-c-i-l-l-y."

"And if the 'c' is not pronounced, is it not silly to have the letter in the word?"

"I thought the same, when I was a child," said Miss Eppel. "My memories of the Isles of Scilly changed during the war."

"You were there during the Second World War, too?" asked Rubles.

"No, dear. But my young man . . ." Miss Eppel looked flustered. "But you were about to tell us your story, Mr. Bernfeld. Don't let me interrupt you."

"I'm sure your story is just as interesting, Miss Eppel," said Ronny, graciously. "Ours will take only a few minutes to tell, so we'll hear yours afterward." He then looked over at his wife. "Shall I tell it, Rubles, or do you want to?"

"You start, dear, and I'll stop you when you make a mistake."

"As I was saying," said Ronny, ignoring his wife's last comment, "today people go to the Isles of Scilly for a holiday by the sea and to see the flowers and wildlife. But during the war, the islands saw plenty of action. Our boys shot down German planes and torpedoed their submarines. And they were ready in case the Germans tried to do a land invasion."

"Where are these islands, exactly?" asked Perlow.

"Off the southwestern tip of

Cornwall, in the Celtic Sea. A few of the islands are inhabited, like St. Mary's and Tresco. But the water is dotted with more than a hundred isles, many of them quite small, that aren't inhabited — at least not officially, if you catch my meaning."

"Ah," said Perlow. "The desolate isle cut off from the mainland, with no means of communication except the occasional ferry that brings supplies and the week-old newspaper — the perfect setting for a mystery story. I am already intrigued."

"So were we," said Rubles, "when we received our assignment."

"Rubles and I were newlyweds during the early years of the war. We had debated whether or not to wait to marry until after the war was over. I wanted to enlist in a combat unit, and I didn't know if it would be fair to Rubles. What if I were killed, or was missing in action? I didn't want to leave my girl a war widow."

"I told Ronny not to be an idiot," said Rubles. "He was the only man for me, so I said that as far as I was concerned it was better to marry and be happy even if it was only for a little while, than not marry and regret it for the rest of my life."

"That was very wise of you," Miss Eppel said softly. Her eyes had gotten misty.

"Is that what happened to you and your young man?"

"Yes, we thought it best to be

prudent. He was in the RAF — one of the few Jews that succeeded in being selected. His plane was shot down over Scilly. Everyone said I would forget him, eventually, and find some other nice young man to marry. I suppose I take things too much to heart, because I never could forget him. As you said, Rubles, he was the only man for me. But I've interrupted your story again, Mr. Bernfeld. Please go on."

"I'm trying to remember where I was," said Ronny.

"You were trying to get into a combat unit, dear, but they thought you could be better used in Army Intelligence."

"That's right. Rubles and I had done a little sleuthing for a chap in the government before the war. Nothing big, you understand, but we'd shown our mettle, shown we could use our wits to get out of a tight jam. So when war broke out and this chap found himself in charge of some Intelligence operations, he thought of me."

"Us, dear." Rubles smiled sweetly at her husband.

"A husband and wife team of spies? Was that not dangerous?" asked Perlow. "Would it not be natural for your first loyalty to be to your spouse and not your country?"

"Oh, they have their ways of vetting a person, Mr. P.," replied Ronny. "But as I was saying, one day we received a visit from this chap — from now on I'll refer to him as 'the Chief,' if you don't mind."

"Surely, you can reveal his name now," said Agatha. "The man has probably been dead for years."

Ronny shrugged. "Better safe than sorry is my motto."

"And it's too bad we never followed it," said Rubles. "But life would have been dull if we had."

"Rubles, I can't get on with the story if you keep interrupting me."

"Sorry, dear. Mum's the word, from now on."

Ronny opened his mouth.

Rubles opened hers, too. "Keep calm and carry on."

Ronny gave her a dirty look. He waited for her to make another comment. When she didn't, he carried on. "So, the Chief showed up at our apartment one day, and he said, 'Bernfeld, I've got a job for you — and the missus, if you both agree.' He told us the bare minimum."

"The top brass were concerned there was some funny business in the Scilly Isles," Rubles explained.

"They thought someone was spying on our troops and passing on the information to the Germans?" asked Miss Eppel.

"Or passing on classified information," Rubles added. 'Signaling with lights, I suppose."

"Such wickedness," said Miss Eppel, shaking her head.

"They had no proof as to who it

was or how many people were involved," said Ronny. "But they had their suspicions. So the Chief said, 'I've arranged for a few persons in Intelligence to take a short holiday on one of the Scilly Islands, a well-deserved rest for valuable service; at least that's what they think they've been invited for. In truth, I want you two to observe them. Take note of what they talk about, the questions they ask, the information they reveal — that sort of thing. Also, some of them haven't met before, so watch out for who strikes up a friendship and who keeps to himself. Keep an eye on where they go, and if they try to contact anyone off the island.'

" 'What's our cover, sir?' I asked.

" 'You and Rubles have been hired to cook and serve the meals and otherwise take care of the guests. You'll make the beds and sweep out the bedrooms, which will give you an opportunity to go through the closets and drawers. You'll wait at table and serve the after-dinner coffee, so you can overhear the conversations. You'll think up chores that need to be done, so it will appear natural for you to be indoors or outdoors, as needed.'

" 'Is there anyone in particular we should keep an eye on?'

" 'There is one, possibly two men who may be traitors. But I'm not going to tell you who they are. If I did, you'd show your hand.' When

Rubles opened her mouth to protest, the Chief said, 'You wouldn't do it on purpose, Mrs. Ronny. But the person would know. He'd sense it. And the scheme would be a failure. Well? Are you game?'

"We didn't hesitate. We accepted the commission.

" 'I knew I could depend on you two,' said the Chief. 'The house on the island has already been supplied with everything you need in terms of food and drink. The linens have been freshly washed, and the house has been aired out and cleaned. When you arrive, all you need to do is prepare the first meal. But don't be wasteful with the food. After the ferryman drops off you and the guests on the island, he won't return for a week. There's no telephone or radio receiver on the island, so you won't be able to make contact with the mainland. And please do be careful. If the person realizes we're on to him, he might turn dangerous. I think that's all, except for one last thing. If they ask why you haven't enlisted or been drafted, Bernfeld, it's because you had rheumatic fever as a child and it left you with a weak heart.'

" 'Yes, sir. When do we leave?'

" 'Tomorrow. I assume you have a black dress you can wear, Mrs. Ronny?'

" 'I've used that disguise before,' Rubles said. 'I have everything I need.'

" 'I forgot about something, sir.

Chanukah starts tomorrow night. It's a Jewish holiday. We have to light candles for eight days. Will that be a problem?'

" 'Not at all, Bernfeld. All of the guests are Jewish, too.'

"Rubles and I were speechless. Then Rubles said, 'There must be some mistake. What Jew would spy for the Germans?'

"At first, I thought the Chief was joking," said Ronny. "But he was deadly serious. 'I hope I am wrong,' he told us. 'But this is war, and we can't take chances.'

"Knowing we would be spying on other Jews dampened our enthusiasm. But we had agreed to do the job, and we were determined to do the best job we could. I won't bore you with details about the next day and our travels. It was only when we were on the ferry to our island that we got a glimpse of the guests. There was a cold wind blowing and the sea was choppy, so no one spoke much. Each of us sat with shoulders hunched against the wind and hats drawn low on our faces.

"I think we were all relieved when we finally reached shore, even though the island didn't look particularly inviting. Perhaps in the summer it was different. But in the cold late afternoon light, the house, which sat on top of a steep hill, had a silent, sinister look to it, as though evil had been done there before — and might be done again."

"I don't mind saying," said Rubles, "that when I looked back and saw the ferry disappearing from view, I almost ran down to the pier to call the ferryman back."

"The house had been furnished with an eye to comfort, although since there was no central heating all the rooms were freezing cold," said Ronny. "I'll say this for the six men who had been invited, they weren't snobs or complainers. They agreed to get the fire going in the sitting room, while Rubles and I got to work in the kitchen. The house was much too big for Rubles and I to take care of everything."

"Perhaps now is the time to give us the names of the six men, Monsieur Bernfeld," said Perlow, "and a brief description."

"I won't give you their real names. Some of them may still be alive. Rubles, you're better at making up names than I am. Change the army ranks, too."

Rubles took up the cue. "Let me see. First, there was Major Sterne. That's rather a good name for him. He was an older man; at least he seemed so at the time, although he probably wasn't a day older than 45. I don't think he relaxed the entire time. Next, there was Dr. Smiles. He was a medical doctor in civilian life. He was one of those avuncular, jolly types, although he did have a temper when he'd had too much to drink. Apparently, he knew, fluently, a dozen European languages, which was why he was drafted into Army Intelligence.

"The youngest person there, besides Ronny and me, was Harry Walker. He was one of those brilliant but socially awkward types, even around men. He liked to take long walks by himself. I believe his job was breaking codes. Geoffrey Rich was only a little older than Harry, but the total opposite. He was urbane, Cambridge educated and had obviously been born with the proverbial silver spoon in his mouth. He was also handsome as anything. I never found out what he actually did in the army, although I had my suspicions.

"The fifth guest didn't have such a vivid personality, so he is a bit harder to type. I'll call him Simon Says, because he pretty much went along with whatever was suggested. He had golden hands, though, and he could fix just about anything. He worked with equipment, fixing and building the snooping devices. Lastly, there was David Polsky. He was in his late twenties and he had very sad eyes. He was from Warsaw, but he was visiting in England when war broke out. He also knew several languages, which is why he was allowed to do army work, I suppose." She then added, "How'd I do, Monsieur Perlow?"

Perlow smoothed down his hair. It bounced back up. "I take off my hat to you, Madame Rubles. Your descriptions had order and method.

Let us now proceed. Monsieur Bernfeld."

"Yes, well, everything was very well organized. There was a notebook with written instructions. In it were which room had been assigned to which person, what times the meals would be served, and things like that. After we had all unpacked and got a few fires going to warm up the public rooms, our instructions were to meet in the sitting room for 'orientation.' There was a gramophone set up in the room, and my instructions were to play the record that had been placed on the record player before our arrival. This wasn't a record with music. It was a man speaking — I didn't recognize the voice. I don't remember all that was said, and later I wished I had been paying more attention, because the record disappeared after that first night. I suppose I was both tired from the traveling and still trying to get the hang of things, which was why my attention wasn't on the recording. But I do remember that the voice welcomed each of the guests by name and said a few words about his background and army career — and that the atmosphere grew tenser as the recording progressed."

"This was your impression as well, Madame Rubles?" asked Perlow.

"I wasn't in the sitting room for orientation. I was in the kitchen.

The plan for the first night was to have an early dinner, after candle lighting, because everyone would probably be tired and hungry."

"Then we must rely upon the impressions of Monsieur Bernfeld."

"I don't see why not," said Ronny. "The Chief did."

"I did not mean to offend, *mon ami.* But the second opinion is often valuable."

"During dinner, the atmosphere was more relaxed," continued Ronny. "The army had stocked the wine cellar with a generous selection of very good wines, and I refilled most of the wine glasses several times. There was also a festive touch for the centerpiece, since it was Chanukah: eight large wooden dreidels. They were the old-fashioned kind. The dreidel itself was made from plain, unpainted wood, while the four Hebrew letters were each painted a different color. I recall that the letter *nun* was painted blue, while the *gimmel* was bright red. Dr. Smiles was the first to reach for one of the dreidels and spin it.

" 'I haven't played dreidel since I was a little boy,' he said, smiling like he was a boy of seven or eight again. 'Shall we have a game after dinner?'

"I should say here that I don't think any of the guests, except Polsky, was a religious Jew. He was the one who said the blessings and lit the one menorah that had been provided for us, while the rest of us said amen. Therefore, none of the others rushed to accept Dr. Smiles's suggestion. When some protested they didn't know how to play the game, the doctor, who was a little tipsy from overindulging in the wine, explained the rules.

" 'A dreidel is a spinning top,' he said. 'So the first rule is that everyone takes a turn spinning it. Now there are four Hebrew letters printed on the dreidel, one on each side, like we have here: *nun, gimmel, hey, shin.* The letters form an ac . . . acro . . . nymonyn . . . You know what I mean. Four letters. *Neis Gadol Hayah Sham* — A Great Miracle Happened There. A miracle. The Maccabees won the war against the Greeks. The little jug of oil lasted for eight days. Everybody is happy. So on Chanukah you have a party and you eat and you play dreidel. You spin the dreidel on the table. If it lands on the *gimmel,* you get *gornisht,* nothing. You don't take and you don't put in. It's like you're dead. You don't exist anymore. *Hey* gets you *halb,* or half. *Shin* is *shtel;* you have to put in. You get *nun,* that's *nemen.* You take it all.'

" 'All of what?' Simon asked, although it's my opinion he was just being polite.

" 'All the money in the pot,' Dr. Smiles replied. 'Children play for nuts or chocolates, but that's no fun for us. I suggest we play for shillings, at least to start.'

" 'You are mistaken, Doctor,' said David Polsky.

" 'Oh?'

" '*Gimmel* does not stand for *gornisht.* It means *gantz.* Everything. When the dreidel lands on *gimmel,* this is when you get all the money. It is *nun* that means *nisht,* or nothing.'

" 'Is that so?' said Dr. Smiles. "Maybe that's how they play dreidel in Warsaw or Krakow or wherever you're from, Mr. Polsky. But in Manchester, which is where I'm from, *gornisht* means *gornisht.* And since we're playing dreidel on English soil . . .'

" 'God save the king,' said Geoffrey Rich, raising his glass. He had also drunk more wine than he should have.

" 'Since this is England,' Dr. Smiles continued, 'you land on *gimmel* and you'll be sorry.'

"Dr. Smiles shook the dreidel in his hand in the direction of Mr. Polsky. His face had turned almost as red as the painted *gimmel*. I don't know why Polsky persisted, since it was obvious Smiles was drunk. Besides, it was only a game they were arguing about. But he did.

" 'That is not how one plays dreidel, Dr. Smiles,' he said, rising from the table. 'If you are as ignorant of the languages you pretend to understand as you are about dreidel, it is we who will be sorry. With translators such as yourself working in Intelligence, next year we will be playing dreidel in a forced labor camp and England will be part of the Third Reich.'

"Polsky stormed out of the room. Dr. Smiles looked like he was going to have an apoplectic fit. For a few tense moments, I thought the doctor was going to challenge Polsky to a duel. Fortunately, Major Sterne put an end to the nonsense.

" 'You've had too much to drink,' " he said to Dr. Smiles. 'Go to bed and sleep it off.'

"It sounded like an order and the doctor obeyed. The others retired early, too, that first night. I know I was glad they did. I was exhausted. Of course, Rubles would want to talk after we went to our room."

"Well, wouldn't you have wanted to talk, too?" Rubles asked the others.

"Oh, yes," Miss Eppel agreed. "I presume Mr. Polsky and Dr. Smiles worked in the same office, which is how he was aware of the mistakes in Dr. Smiles's work."

"Pardon, Miss Eppel," said Perlow, "but it is too early to presume anything. First, we must hear the facts."

"The facts were that the next morning Mr. Polsky didn't come down to breakfast," said Ronny. "What was also strange was that someone had taken six of the dreidels from the centerpiece and put one on each of the guests' plates.

Five of them had the *nun* side up. On Mr. Polsky's plate it was the *gimmel.*"

"It was not you, Madame Rubles, who arranged the table settings?"

"I was in the kitchen, Monsieur Perlow, preparing the food for breakfast. It was Ronny who was in charge of the dining room."

"I wasn't sure if we should bring out the food, or wait for Mr. Polsky," said Ronny. "Once again, it was Major Sterne who took charge. He didn't approve of tardiness, he said. They were still in the army, even if they were on holiday. He went upstairs to reprimand Mr. Polsky. When he returned, his face was ashen.

" 'You'd better come with me, Dr.

Smiles. It appears Mr. Polsky has met with an accident.'

"I won't mention unnecessary details. In short, Mr. Polsky was dead. By his bedside was a glass of water that was about a third full. There was also a bottle of sleeping pills, also only about a third full."

"Dear, dear," said Miss Eppel. "How very tragic."

"Was there a note?" asked Agatha.

"No," replied Ronny. "During breakfast, the others discussed why he might have done it. The consensus was that Mr. Polsky must have been emotionally unbalanced. After all, it was odd that he had gotten so upset about a game of dreidel."

"There was no suspicion that the

good doctor might have had a hand in dispatching Monsieur Polsky to heaven?" asked Perlow.

"No. I mean it would have been too obvious. Someone insults you at dinner. The next day the person dies of an overdose."

"Very true. What did you do with the body?"

"Major Sterne and Simon Says went to hunt up a place to store it, until the ferry returned."

"There was a separate cellar, one that wasn't used to store food," said Rubles. "They put the body there."

"You and Madame Rubles were not involved in the removal of the body?"

"No," said Ronny. "The pipe leading to the kitchen sink had sprung a leak, so we had to take of that. In the end, we had to turn off the water leading to the kitchen and pump water from the well instead."

"Don't forget to tell them about the missing dreidel," said Rubles.

"I haven't forgotten. When the guests gathered for lunch, someone — I think it was Geoffrey Rich — noticed one of the dreidels was missing. There were only seven of them on the table. There were the two still in the center, while the other five had once again been placed on the guests' plates."

"It was Geoffrey," said Rubles. "I remember you telling me afterwards. He counted the dreidels and then he asked everyone what letter they had. The other four said they had a *nun.*"

"That's right," said Ronny. "Then Dr. Smiles asked, 'What about you, Rich?'

" 'This afternoon you must call me something else, Doctor,' Geoffrey said. He then held up his dreidel so the others could see. 'I've got *gornisht.*'

"During lunch it was once again Dr. Smiles who did most of the talking, but it was all pretty much ado about nothing. Everyone was careful not to talk about his work in Intelligence or express an opinion about the way the war effort was being handled. My impression was they were a suspicious lot. Not that I blame them. When you work in Intelligence and know how things are done, you naturally suspect there is a listening device somewhere in the room. I suppose the Chief was hoping the wine served at the meals would loosen up a few tongues.

"Rubles and I spent most of the day in or near the kitchen. It took time to go through all the cupboards and the storage cellar and figure out where everything was. Later in the afternoon dark clouds began to roll in from the sea. I remember remarking to Rubles there would probably be a storm that night, so we'd better make sure we knew where the candles and lanterns were stored, in case the lights went out. Major Sterne had had the same thought. He came to the kitchen with Simon Says and Harry Walker.

" 'Harry and I are going out to the woodshed to chop some more wood,' he told us. "Simon is going to take a look at the generator and get familiar with it.'

" 'That's our job, Major Sterne,' I protested. 'This is supposed to be a holiday for you.'

" 'I don't know what the army was thinking, sending just the two of you to do all the work,' Major Sterne replied. 'It's not your fault if you can't do it all. I shan't give you a bad report, as long as you continue to serve the meals on time.'

"It was a good thing we all made the preparations when we did, because about an hour later a storm unleashed its fury on the island. We were just putting the finishing touches on the first course when the lights began to flicker. Then there was a boom of thunder that made us jump, followed by a flash of lightning so strong the black sky was momentarily lit up like it was daylight.

" 'We'd better light some candles,' I said to Rubles, 'just to be on the safe side.'

"And it's a good thing we didn't wait, because a minute or two later the lights went out. We took the candles with us to the sitting room, where the others had gathered for cocktails before dinner. The lights had gone out there as well, but there was some light in the room, thanks to the fire burning in the fireplace. There was a discussion as to whether to go out and try to fix the generator first, or serve dinner. It was agreed to eat first by candle-light, while the main course was still hot, and then do the repair. We were all turning toward the dining room, when we heard a scream, followed by the sound of a heavy object thumping down the stairs.

"Major Sterne grabbed the candle from Rubles's hand — and I'll say this about the Major, he might have had a desk job, but he didn't have a fearful bone in his body — and he rushed into the dark hallway. Dr. Smiles followed after him. They returned just a few minutes later.

" 'It's Rich,' said Major Sterne. 'His candle must have blown out while he was coming down the stairs.'

" 'Is he all right, sir?' I said.

" 'No, he's not all right. He's dead. He broke his neck.' Major Sterne asked Harry Walker to help him move Mr. Rich's body back to his bedchamber. Because there were no lights, it was too dangerous to take the body down to the cellar, where the corpse of Mr. Polsky was being stored. And it seemed that Dr. Smiles wasn't able to help, because of a bad back.

"While they were removing the body, Simon Says said to me, 'Give me your candle. I'm going out to the shed to fix the generator. It's not safe wandering around in this big house without light.'

"We didn't like being left alone without a candle, but there was some light from the fireplace and so we weren't exactly frightened."

"To be exact, we were petrified," said Rubles. She then said to her husband, "Don't play the hero, Ronny. Anyone would have been terrified, what with the storm, the two deaths — and the feeling there was something strange going on, under the surface."

"Rubles is right," said Ronny. "We were both starting to get the creeps. You understand there was nothing out of the ordinary about the two deaths. People do take an overdose of sleeping tablets. People do fall down stairs and break their neck. But we couldn't help wondering, what's going to happen next?

"After Major Sterne, Dr. Smiles and Harry Walker came back downstairs, we all went into the dining room. Major Sterne gave us one of the candles, so Rubles and I could go into the kitchen and dish out the food. One of the candles remained in the dining room, so the guests wouldn't have to sit in the dark. I immediately lit several of the other candles we had prepared beforehand and took one of the candelabras into the dining room. In the end there was no need for it, because the lights came back on.

"Major Sterne looked about the room. 'Simon went out to the

shed?' he asked me.

" 'Yes, sir.'

" 'His orders were to wait until after we had dined.'

"I didn't say anything. It wasn't my place to respond, not in my guise as a hired servant.

" 'The table is missing another dreidel,' Harry Walker said.

"We looked around. The two dreidels sitting in the middle of the table, as a sort of centerpiece, were still there. But although there were five place settings on the table — I had set the table before Mr. Rich met with his accident — there were dreidels on only four of the plates.

" 'I've got a *nun,*' said Dr. Smiles. 'What about you, Walker?'

"Harry Walker looked down at his

place setting. Then he looked at the setting next to his. 'It's Simon,' he said. 'He's got the *gimmel.*'

" 'Why hasn't he returned?' Major Sterne muttered. I could see that even he was starting to feel unnerved.

" 'Shall I got out to the shed and fetch him, sir?' Walker asked.

" 'I'll go with you,' said Major Sterne, rising from his seat. As I think I mentioned, in his own way Major Sterne was a man of action. I suppose in his earlier days he had received a wound that prevented him from returning to the battlefield. But I remember thinking that if I ever did see active service I'd want to serve under a commander like him.

"But to get back to the story, Dr. Smiles was starting to pour himself a glass of wine, when the Major said, 'You may as well come, too, Doctor Smiles, in case we need you.'

"They went out to the shed. I suppose you can guess what happened next."

"They discovered the body of Monsieur Says," said Perlow.

"That's right. His head had been bashed in. Apparently a heavy object had fallen off a shelf, while Simon was leaning over the generator. It could have been an 'act of nature,' at least that's what Dr. Smiles thought had happened. The shed was rather flimsily built. The strong winds might have caused things on the shelf to move."

"But you, Monsieur Bernfeld, you were not entirely satisfied?"

"No, Mr. P., and neither were the others. The conversation at table, when they returned to the dining room, was somber. At least the conversation between Major Sterne and Harry Walker was.

" 'I don't like it, sir,' Walker said.

" 'No one likes death,' Major Sterne replied.

" 'I wouldn't say no one, Major," said Dr. Smiles, chuckling. 'For a physician, illness and death are his bread and butter.'

" 'None of these men were ill,' said Walker. 'And if you say they died a natural death, I say . . .'

"He paused and looked at the

other two men. 'Well, what do you say?' asked Dr. Smiles. The wine was beginning to make him truculent again.

" 'I say they were murdered.'

"Dr. Smiles laughed. 'Ridiculous. You've probably read too many of those mystery stories.'

" 'Are you suggesting one of us is a murderer?' asked Major Sterne.

"Walker looked uneasy. 'Not one of us, perhaps, but what about them?' He cast a dark look in my direction. 'We don't know anything about Carstairs here and his wife.'

"I'm sure I don't have to explain that Rubles and I were going under the name of Mr. and Mrs. Carstairs for this job."

"There always seems to be someone named Carstairs in a mystery story," said Miss Eppel, rather dreamily. "Yet one rarely meets a Carstairs in real life."

"I once knew a Carstairs," said Agatha, feeling rather defensive because she had used the name more than once in her mystery novels. "Blanche Carstairs. She had a dress shop in town. Of course she didn't call herself Carstairs. Everyone had to sound like they were French in those days. I believe she went by the name Madame Blanc. But I can assure you she was a real flesh-and-blood person and not a figment of my imagination."

"Well, Rubles and I were good old-fashioned English Carstairs," said Ronny. "And we didn't like it one bit when Walker suggested we were the ones responsible for the deaths of Simon, Rich and Polsky.

" 'You're mad, man,' Dr. Smiles said to Walker. 'If there is a maniac loose on this island, it isn't one of us. I'd bet money on that.'

" 'How can you be so sure?' asked Walker.

" 'Carstairs and his missus were in the sitting room with us, when Rich fell down the stairs, weren't they?'

"Walker was forced to admit this was true. 'If one death was an accident, there's no reason to jump to the conclusion that the other two were not.' Dr. Smiles poured another glass of wine and drank it down in one gulp. When he pushed the bottle in Walker's direction, the young man said, 'No thanks. I'd rather keep my mind clear, from now on.'

"Nothing out of the ordinary happened the next day. Although the guests approached the dining room with some hesitancy at breakfast, you could feel the relief in the air when each place setting had a dreidel on it and each dreidel had been placed *nun* side up. The day was fine — it was hard to imagine there had been a terrific storm the night before — and Walker said he intended to go for a walk. Major Sterne had brought along a manuscript he was working on. If I recall correctly, he had an interest in medieval enamels and he was writing a monograph on the topic. Although I didn't see this with my own eyes, I believe our Doctor Smiles had taken a bottle of whisky somewhere and was getting quietly drunk alone.

"I wanted to follow Harry Walker. I was still miffed that he had accused Rubles and me the night before, and I would have loved to catch him building a bonfire on the beach and signaling to someone on another island. But Rubles had cut her hand while chopping vegetables for lunch, and she needed me to finish the job. Neither of us was able to leave the kitchen area all morning.

"At lunch, when the three men gathered in the dining room, I

sensed there was once again a feeling of relief. Just as the rainstorm
had passed outside and left only
sunshine in its wake, the spate of
accidents inside the house also
seemed to be a thing of the past.
But at dinner the old tricks began
again. This time it was Walker who
got the *gimmel.*

"Oh, dear," murmured Miss Eppel. "How did the young man die?"

"None of us heard him, but apparently he went back outside in
the middle of the night. We found
his body the next morning, at the
bottom of a cliff. He might have
lost his footing in the dark, while
walking on the cliff, and fallen off."

"Or he was pushed," said Miss
Eppel, shaking her head. "There is

such wickedness in the world."

"You say 'we,' Monsieur Bernfeld. Does that mean you were part of the search party and saw the body lying there with your own eyes?"

"No, Mr. P.," said Ronny. "By this point, I didn't like to leave Rubles alone in the house."

Rubles put her hand on her husband's arm. "Thank you, dear."

"So now there were just you and Rubles and the Major and the Doctor," said Perlow.

"That's right. They hadn't eaten breakfast before they went out to look for Walker. Even though no one was hungry, after they disposed of the body Dr. Smiles suggested they should eat something.

" 'If Walker was right and there is

a maniac running loose, we need to keep our strength up,' he said.

" 'Very well,' said Major Sterne. He then nodded in my direction and said, 'You may serve breakfast now.'

" 'And I suggest Carstairs and his wife eat their meals with us, here in this room,' said Dr. Smiles. When Major Sterne raised an eyebrow, the doctor explained, 'I don't believe for a minute they are killers and would try to poison us, but it's better to be safe than sorry. If they're eating the same food as us, we'll all rest easier.'

"It made sense, but in the end, it didn't help him. At dinner, Dr. Smiles got the *gimmel.* He died of a heart attack that night in his sleep. And this time I did see the body, Mr. P. I'm not a doctor, but he looked dead to me.

"When we sat down to breakfast, Major Sterne was looking grim. He took up the dreidel sitting on his plate and gave it a spin. Don't get me wrong, it wasn't a playful spin. Nor was there a crazed look in his eyes.

"When the dreidel fell on the letter *shin,* which if you'll recall means you put a coin in the pot, he stared at the dreidel and said, as though talking to the dreidel and not to us, 'All right. I'll put in my opinion. I don't know how you two escaped being accurately vetted by Intelligence, but you did it. I also don't know what your paymasters back in Germany hope to get out of all this. Even though you'll have murdered the six of us, we're only a drop in the Intelligence bucket. The British Army has plenty more at work on breaking your codes and monitoring your communications. I'd say they're just as smart, if not smarter, than the six of us who were sent to this island. I'll also say that if you think you can scare me and make me give away whatever secrets I may know, you are mistaken. So let's get it over with.'

"Major Sterne removed a revolver from the inside pocket of his jacket and pushed the revolver in my direction. I looked down at it with horror. 'We're not spies,' I assured him. I pushed the gun back in his direction."

"That wasn't very bright of you, dear," said Rubles.

"I know, dear. You don't have to always remind me."

"So the good Major picked up the revolver?" asked Perlow. "And he aimed it at you, *n'est-ce pas*?"

"First he aimed it at me," said Ronny. We sat looking at each other for a few minutes. When neither one of us blinked, as the saying goes, he said, 'All right, Carstairs, I believe you're telling the truth. You're not a German spy.'

"I was in the middle of breathing a sigh of relief, when he aimed the gun at Rubles instead. 'That leaves you, Mrs. Carstairs.'

Ronny looked over at his wife.

"Rubles, do you want to tell this part of the story?"

"You bet I do. I was shocked when he said that, and I said so. 'It's you who are the spy, isn't it, Major Sterne? You knew Army Intelligence was getting suspicious. That's why you killed the others, so they couldn't find you out. And I suppose after you kill Ronny and me, you're going to slip away to some German boat docked somewhere on this island and try to make it back to Germany.'

" 'Nice try, Mrs. Carstairs. A very nice try. But if there is a boat on this island, it's here to ferry you back to Germany.'

"I didn't like my wife being accused of being a spy," said Ronny, "so I said, 'My wife isn't a spy, Major Sterne. I can understand you being nervous, after all that's happened here. But I can vouch for Rubles . . .'

" 'Rubles?'

" 'It's just a nickname, sir,' I said. 'Her real name is Rose.'

"Such an old-fashioned name," Rubles said to the others. "I never liked it."

" 'I beg your pardon, Mrs. Carstairs,' said Major Sterne. "I see you are not a German spy. You are spying for the Russians.'

" 'You don't understand,' Rubles said. 'I'm not a spy and my husband isn't a spy. Rubles is the name my grandfather used to call me. He was born in Russia and could barely speak English. He always used to tell me a good woman was more precious than diamonds, or even rubles — but if you had the choice take the diamonds, because a ruble wasn't worth much in those days. And then he'd laugh. It was only a joke.'

" 'You might want to leave the room, Carstairs,' said Major Sterne. 'This won't be pretty.'

"Major Sterne cocked the revolver," said Ronny. "I couldn't believe this was happening to us. I thought it was only in thriller novels that the protagonists were so dumb they fell straight into the enemy's trap. I was trying to think of what I could do to divert Sterne's attention while I made a move to get the revolver away from him. But he had the revolver aimed at Rubles's head and his hand was steady. He was ready to shoot.

" 'Are you leaving or staying?' he said, not looking in my direction. His eyes were fastened upon Rubles.

" 'Ronny, do something. He's going to do it. He's going to kill me!'

" 'Don't listen to her, Carstairs. She's a spy all right. She's the reason why all of us were sent to this island. It was to find her.'

" 'You knew about the mission, sir?'

" 'Of course, I did. I thought we were after Smiles. I thought that was why we were sent to Scilly. But I was wrong. Mrs. Carstairs killed

Polsky to cast suspicion on the doctor.'

" 'Don't believe him, Ronny. He's lying. I didn't kill Mr. Polsky. I've never killed anyone. You believe me, don't you, Ronny? Ronny!'

" 'I . . . I . . .'

" 'If you want to clear your name, Bernfeld, so there's no doubt . . .'

" 'You . . . you know my real name, sir?'

" 'I told you, Bernfeld, I'm in on the show, too. If you want to go home with a record that's squeaky clean, you'll do as I say. Stand up, slowly, and leave the room.'

"I hesitated. A dozen thoughts were flashing through my mind. I loved Rubles more than anything in the world. But I knew her grandfather and her father were die-hard socialists. I'd always assumed they just wanted better rights for workers, but that they were loyal British subjects. But could I say, without a doubt, that this was so?

"Major Sterne was getting impatient. 'That's an order, Bernfeld,' he said. 'You'll thank me later. Get out of the room.'

"The truth crashed down on me like a load of bricks. 'Oh, God!' I cried out. 'I'm married to a Russian agent!'

"I rushed out of the room, despite Sterne's orders to walk slowly. The kitchen door slammed behind me. I heard the gunshot. I heard Rubles's body fall on the floor with a loud thump. And then I heard the door to the kitchen creak open, slowly. I turned. Sterne was standing in the doorway. In one hand he still held the revolver. In the other he held a dreidel. Both the gun and the *gimmel* were pointed at me.

" 'It's your turn, Bernfeld,' Sterne said, as calmly as ever.

" 'But . . . I . . . I thought you said,' I stammered. 'I'm innocent. I tell you, I'm innocent!'

" 'There are only the two of us left.'

"For the first time, I saw Major Sterne smile. It wasn't a pleasant sight. In a sudden flash, I realized the truth. He had played me like the naïve lad that I was. Of course, Rubles was innocent! And I had left her to die at this madman's hand.

"I tried to stay calm, but to stay calm and carry on is easier said than done when a madman is pointing a gun at your head.

" 'You won't get away with this, Sterne,' I said, trying to sound braver than I felt. 'There's a listening device installed over there, behind the bread box. It's recording everything we're saying.'

"I'd hoped Sterne would at least glance over at the counter. Even a few seconds would have given me time to rush him and try to grab the revolver. But he just laughed.

" 'The only listening device on this island is the hearing aid in Smiles's ear. The game's over, Bernfeld. I suggest you say your prayers, before you're . . .'

"The last things I remember hearing, before I hit the floor, were the gunshot and . . . *gornisht!*"

"You died? No, of course you didn't die," said Agatha. "My head is in a muddle. I must have been thinking of something else, some other story."

"When I woke up," Ronny continued, "I was lying on the settee in the sitting room. A familiar voice was saying, 'That's better, Bernfeld. Try sitting up, if you can.'

" 'Chief?' I mumbled. My head wasn't entirely clear. When I fell, it must have gotten a good *klop*. But I saw that I could sit up and so I did. But when I looked around the room, I was certain I had fainted a second time. What I was seeing couldn't possibly be true. They were all there, smiling at me — Rubles and Major Sterne and Dr. Smiles. Walker, Rich and Polsky were there, too.

" 'Don't be amazed, Bernfeld,' said the Chief. 'I'm sorry I had to put you through all this, but Major Sterne, who is my chief, wasn't convinced you would be able to handle the real assignment I intended to give you and Mrs. Ronny. We weren't sure what you would do, if your wife was captured by the enemy. Would you crack under the stress and divulge what you knew, to gain her safety, or would you remain calm and put your loyalty to your country first. So we had to devise this little show.'

" 'It looks like I failed, sir. I cracked, and nearly cracked my head open on that stone floor, so I guess I'm not much use to my country. And I was willing to let someone kill my wife, so I guess I've failed as a human being, too.'

" 'Nonsense,' said Major Sterne. 'You did better than most chaps would in the same situation. As far as I'm concerned, you've passed the test. I know. I've put on this little show before. The dreidel business took some practice, since I wasn't familiar with the Hebrew alphabet, but your wife helped by checking up on me, to see that everyone got the right letter.'

" 'You mean you were in on it, too?' I asked Rubles.

" 'Of course I was, Ronny. Why else would I have broken the water pipe, cut my hand, and played dead when Major Sterne supposedly shot me?'

"I was still trying to take this all in, when Major Sterne said, 'You're ready for your next assignment, Bernfeld. The real one.'

" 'Thank you, sir, but there's not going to be a next assignment.'

" 'Why not?' asked the Chief.

" 'Rubles and I have always worked as a team, sir. I can't imagine going it alone. She's the one with the brains, the one who gets us out when we're in a jam. I don't think she'd want to work with me ever again, not after I left her in the lurch, to face her fate alone.'

"Rubles came over to the settee and sat down beside me. Then she leaned over and gave me a kiss on the cheek.

" 'Nonsense,' she told me. 'I'd do the same for you any time.' "

THE OLIVE
CRACKED

"Well, ducks, who's for dessert?" The waitress grinned at them. She was from the old school, Agatha noted. There were no pretensions about her. She saw herself as a mother goose who had to lead her wandering ducklings through the meal, so the kitchen staff could get on with cleaning up at a reasonable hour and the residents could take an after-lunch nap or retire to one of the public rooms with a newspaper and a cup of tea or coffee.

An idea popped into Agatha Krinsky's head.

"Is it possible to serve our dessert and coffee somewhere else?" she asked. "Such as the . . . library?"

"What a nice idea," murmured Miss Eppel.

"A change of scenery is often good for the digestion," agreed Herschel Perlow. You permit, madame?"

The waitress hesitated. Then she said, "Why not? It's Chanukah, isn't it? You run along to the library, and I'll send up the dessert things on a trolley."

Running was out of the question. But a few members of the group hurried to retrieve their walking aids. Agatha needed her walker.

Both Herschel Perlow and Miss Eppel used a cane. There was an awkward moment when Miss Eppel dropped her bag with her crocheting things, and several crochet hooks dropped on the floor and rolled away. Fortunately, both Ronny and Rubles Bernfeld were still agile and able to walk unaided. Ronny dropped to his knees to retrieve the fallen hooks. Getting back up was another thing.

"Give us a hand, Rubles," he called out, placing one hand on the table to steady himself and reaching out the other to his wife.

"Heave, ho!" Rubles called out in turn. Ronny made it back up to a standing position without accident.

There was just enough room in

the elevator for all of them. They had only to go to the next floor.

"I've been admiring your jumper all through lunch," Rubles said to Agatha. "Did you make it?"

"No, I haven't a talent for that sort of thing. Not like Miss Eppel."

Miss Eppel's cheeks turned pink. "It's really rather easy to crochet, Mrs. Krinsky, especially when all one does is crochet baby blankets."

The elevator door opened and the group proceeded down the corridor.

"You make an awful lot of them," said Rubles. "Are they for children in your own family, or do you donate them?"

"Neither," replied Miss Eppel. "When I'm done with one, I unravel it and use the yarn again."

"Why bother to do it, then?" asked Agatha.

"Crocheting baby blankets is rather like pretending to be a little deaf in both ears. People tend to avoid you, fearing you'll start to talk about how clever your fifty-seven great-grandchildren are — each and every one of them — and not give them a chance to talk. The pretending to be a little deaf also protects you from bores who retell the same stories again and again. People get tired of having to shout."

"I suppose that's a problem in a place like this," said Agatha. "There are only so many memories a person can have, so many subjects to talk about."

"Of course, people do come and go," said Rubles. "I don't mean to sound crass, but no one lives forever."

They had arrived at the door to the library. Ronny opened it. He and Perlow allowed the ladies to enter the room first.

"This is such a nice room," said Rubles. "I don't know why we don't think to sit here more often."

"There's a draft, as I recall," said Miss Eppel, moving toward the fireplace. "I wonder if we can ask someone to light a fire."

Agatha was trying to move the group closer to the Turkish carpet by the window, where the body had been lying earlier in the day, but all the others were gravitating toward the fireplace. She therefore left the group and started walking toward the window. She wondered if she should pretend to stumble upon the body, as though seeing it for the first time. Although she had mentioned the body's presence several times during lunch, no one had paid her much attention. In the end, she decided not to pretend. It was better to tell the truth. When the police came and began asking questions, her story would be straightforward.

"Oh, look," said Agatha, trying to sound nonchalant. "The dead body is still here."

"What did you say, dear?" asked Miss Eppel, cupping a hand to her ear.

"The dead body. The one I mentioned at lunch. I don't think it's moved since this morning."

"Dead bodies don't usually move, Mrs. Krinsky," said Ronny, "unless someone moves them."

"Who is it?" asked Rubles.

"I don't know," said Agatha. "Perhaps you'd like to come here and see for yourself."

Rubles shuddered. "I'd rather not. It's so difficult when one of the residents passes away, especially if it's someone you like."

"This person looks very young," said Agatha. "I do think we should . . ."

"Here you are, ducks." The waitress had arrived, with a trolley. "Why don't you all find a comfortable chair, and I'll bring you your hot drinks and one of these nice donuts. Let me see, Mr. Perlow, you take coffee, don't you? And Miss Eppel you like a nice cup of Earl Grey tea."

The waitress prepared the hot drinks and served them to the four residents whose tastes she was familiar with. When it was Agatha's turn, she said, "And what about you, ducks? Tea or coffee?"

"Coffee, please," said Agatha, "with one sugar."

The waitress poured out the coffee. She then approached Agatha with the coffee mug in one hand and a plate with a donut on it in the other. "Here you are . . ."

At last, Agatha received what she

felt was an appropriate response to her discovery. The waitress screamed and promptly dropped the mug and the plate on the floor. People began to pour into the room with surprising rapidity. Agatha had no idea who most of them were. But the pandemonium was most gratifying.

Inspector Haddock sat in one of the grandfather chairs. The chair was upholstered with a powder-blue fabric that brought out the blue in his eyes. They were nice eyes, Agatha thought, and they reminded her of someone she knew. It was such a bother to forget things all the time.

"You say you were on your way

to the dining room when you first encountered the body, Mrs. Krinsky?"

Agatha, who was sitting in a matching grandfather chair, said, "I thought that was where I was going, but I lost my way. I only moved to Barnet Court this morning. What a long day it has been."

The fingerprint man whispered something in Inspector Haddock's ear. The Inspector excused himself and went with the fingerprint man to the windowsill. The police surgeon was still conducting his examination of the body and other officers were doing their work of photographing and examining the room for clues, but the crowd of onlookers had been shooed away.

Agatha was the first to be interviewed, and she was surprised by how nervous she felt. Even though she knew she hadn't committed the murder, she also knew that the person who discovered the body was, more often than not, the one who had committed the crime. At least, that's how it was in mystery novels.

Inspector Haddock returned to his chair. "Now, Mrs. Krinsky, you were saying?"

"I was saying that I got off on the wrong floor. Instead of getting off on the first floor, where the dining room is located, I got off on the second floor, with some other people."

"Did you know these people?"

"No."

"Did you all go in the same direction, down the same corridor?"

"No. They turned to the right. I recalled that Sandra had told me earlier the dining room was on the left."

"That would be Sandra Carstairs, Barnet Court's business manager?"

"Is that what she does here? I thought she had something to do with admissions."

"It's possible she was filling in for someone," said Inspector Haddock. "I suppose she asked you to sign some papers?"

"She said I could come to her office after lunch. I believe she said she would be there until four o'clock."

"I suppose you wanted someone to be with you, to also look over the papers — a relative perhaps?"

"My nephew Sheldon was here this morning, to help me with the move. But he couldn't stay. And his wife Jean, who is a lawyer, had looked over the papers the other day. In her opinion, they were quite all right."

"So you turned to the left. Then what happened?"

Agatha explained how she had entered the library, found it a charming room, and began to look around. "Then I saw the body of that young woman. It was horrible. I screamed."

"Did you recognize the woman?"

"No, as I mentioned earlier, I

only arrived here this morning. The only staff member I had met so far was Miss Carstairs."

"Yet you just referred to the body you saw on the carpet as a young woman. How did you know she was young? She was lying on the floor, on her stomach, you know. Unless you moved her."

"I didn't touch a thing. I've been writing mystery stories for over fifty years. That much I know."

A light of recognition began to show in the Inspector's blue eyes. "You mean you're *the* Agatha Krinsky, the famous mystery writer?"

Agatha made the usual incoherent half-sentences she used when people discovered who she was. Despite being famous for most of her life, she had never been comfortable when in the limelight.

"My grandfather, Sir Harold Withering, thought very highly of your books."

"I knew you reminded me of someone, Inspector. You have the same eyes. How is dear Sir Harold? He helped me more than once with some technical questions I had about the inner workings of Scotland Yard."

"My grandfather passed away six months ago."

"Of course. I'm so sorry. One forgets things when one reaches a certain age."

"But you're positive the body you saw this morning is the same body you saw after lunch?"

"Certainly. The body was dressed in the same red dress and was wearing the same black gloves, the same black stockings and shoes, and the same black beret on the same blond hair. She also had the same striped silk scarf tied about her neck."

"But you never actually saw her face?"

"No." Agatha shuddered. "I supposed the poor thing had been strangled, and I didn't like to see . . . I never wrote all the gory details in my novels. But I see what you mean. She might not have been young at all. Some women of forty can pass for twenty-five from the back, if they're slim. It's the face that never lies."

"One last question, Mrs. Krinsky, and then you can return to your room. Why didn't you telephone the police immediately?"

"I wanted to, but no one would listen to me. It was most frustrating. Such a thing would never happen in one of my mystery novels."

"I understand. If I have more questions later, I'll let you know."

"Is it all right if I remain in the room, Inspector? I hate to sound ghoulish, but I do rather feel that this is my body."

"As you wish."

Inspector Haddock was once again needed, this time by the police surgeon. Agatha raised herself from the "hot seat," where she supposed others would be interviewed, and found a place to stand off to the side. A few moments later a commotion was heard outside the door, which was then flung open.

"You can't go in there, sir," a young policeman was saying. "Ma'am, you have to wait outside. You, too, ma'am! Ma'am!"

Inspector Haddock had turned to see who was causing the ruckus. He immediately came forward to halt the progression of the four elderly people who had entered the room.

"I'm terribly sorry," he said, "but this room is off-limits at the moment. We'll try to finish our work here as soon as possible."

Herschel Perlow stepped forward. "Inspector, this is why we have deranged your young assistant at the door. We have come to help you."

"That's very good of you, Mr. . . ."

"Perlow. Herschel Perlow, at your service." Perlow handed the Inspector a business card.

Inspector Haddock glanced at the card. Then he studied it more closely. "Private detective? Your name does sound familiar."

Herschel Perlow smoothed down his hair. It bounced up again.

"Aren't you the fellow from Spain? My late grandfather mentioned you several times."

"Ukraine, Inspector. I am from the Galicia that is in Ukraine." It was obvious that Perlow's feelings had been hurt.

"What about the rest of you?" Inspector Haddock asked the others. "Are you also from Ukraine?"

"I should say not," replied Rubles.

"Rubles and I are strictly British," said Ronny.

"Then why is your name Rubles?"

"It's a long story, Inspector," said Rubles. "Some other time."

"And who are you?" he asked Miss Eppel.

"I knew your late grandfather, Inspector Haddock. Sir Harold was good enough to seek my advice on a few of his cases. It was most gratifying to be asked, although the facts were so obvious that anyone who had been a member of a synagogue Sisterhood could have come up with the right solution."

"Miss Eppel?" Inspector Haddock blinked his eyes several times. "I thought you were . . . I mean . . ."

"Yes, dear, I am ancient. We are all sadly past our prime, I'm afraid. But we would like to help. If we won't be in the way, that is."

A man brushed past the policeman standing at the door and strode over to Inspector Haddock. His dress and manner suggested authority, although his gait was slightly unsteady.

"Inspector Haddock?"

The Inspector nodded. "And you are, sir?"

"Martin Clegg. I'm the manager of Barnet Court. What's all this about?"

Inspector Haddock glanced down at his notebook. "Your secretary said you had a luncheon date in town. Is that correct, sir?"

"That's right. I returned as soon as I received the message."

It was apparent from the manager's red cheeks that his lunch had been accompanied by an ample amount of alcoholic refreshment. But he had not drunk so much that he had lost control of his speech or thought processes, Inspector Haddock noticed.

"I hope you don't mind if I ask you a few questions, sir."

"Of course not," replied Mr. Clegg. "Would you like to come to my office?"

"That will be fine."

Clegg glanced over to where Herschel Perlow, Miss Eppel and Ronny and Rubles were standing. "I really don't think it's appropriate for the residents to hang around here, Inspector," he said quietly. "Some of them have weak hearts, you know."

"I'll ask my people to clear the room." Inspector Haddock motioned for Mr. Clegg to show the way to his office. As they passed Agatha, the Inspector said, "Perhaps you'd like to come with us downstairs, Mrs. Krinsky. We can show you the way to Miss Carstairs's office, so you can sign those papers. Unless, that is, you'd rather go to your room and rest."

Agatha was about to reply that

she'd rather remain where she was, when she thought she saw Inspector Haddock wink at her. At least she thought it was a wink. She didn't have her glasses with her, and so she couldn't be really sure.

"Thank you, Inspector, I will come with you."

While the three walked to the elevator, Mrs. Krinsky made the acquaintance of Mr. Clegg.

"I hope this hasn't given you a bad impression of Barnet Court," he told her. "We don't usually have dead bodies lying about here. This is highly unusual, in fact."

"I understand, Mr. Clegg."

"I'm positive there must be some mistake."

"I don't think so," said Agatha.

"She looked quite dead to me when I found her."

"I don't doubt that. I mean there must be some mistake about how she got here. I understand she wasn't one of the staff, or a relative of one of the residents."

He had asked the question of the Inspector, and it was Inspector Haddock who replied. "At the moment, it's still a mystery as to what she was doing here. But I hope to have that cleared up very soon."

"I hope so, too, Inspector." Clegg then turned to Agatha. "And I do hope you aren't thinking of bolting, Mrs. Krinsky. We are honored you chose to live at Barnet Court."

They had reached the entrance to the administrative offices. To get to

Martin Clegg's office they had to pass by the office of Sandra Carstairs.

"Have you a minute, Sandra?" asked Mr. Clegg. "Mrs. Krinsky would like to sign those papers now."

Sandra Carstairs glanced from Martin Clegg to Agatha to Inspector Haddock. "There's really no rush, Mrs. Krinsky," she said. "If you'd rather wait until tomorrow, after things have settled down, that will be fine."

"Mrs. Krinsky is here now," said Mr. Clegg. While his tone was still friendly, it was also firm. Inspector Haddock wondered if the manager really was afraid that Mrs. Krinsky and possibly the others would leave the facility, either because of the shock from there having been a murder on the premises or the scandal.

Sandra still hesitated. Then her face relaxed into a smile. "Please have a seat, Mrs. Krinsky. This will only take a few minutes."

Clegg was leaving the business manager's office, satisfied that his orders were being followed. "My office is just a few steps away, Inspector."

Inspector followed him to the doorway. Then he suddenly turned around. Sandra Carstairs was in the middle of placing a folder on the desk, in front of Agatha. He quickly returned to the desk and snatched up the folder. "Thank you, Miss Carstairs. I'll take that, if you don't mind."

"I'm sorry, but I still don't understand," said Agatha. "I'm afraid too much has happened today."

"Do not apologize, madame," said Monsieur Perlow. "We shall go over it again — this time with order and method." He gave Inspector Haddock a disapproving look.

"I seem to have dropped my crochet hook again," said Miss Eppel.

"Don't worry," said Ronny, rising from his chair.

"Ronny, I don't think you should bend down twice in one day," said Rubles. "My back can't take the strain."

"I'll get it," said a young blond-haired woman, who was wearing a red dress and a black beret. She retrieved the hook, which had rolled beside her chair, and gave it back to Miss Eppel.

"Thank you, dear," Miss Eppel murmured.

They were all seated in the library. The tea trolley had been replenished with coffee, tea, and donuts with blue icing, in honor of Chanukah. It was all very cozy. It was also still more than a little bewildering for Agatha, who kept staring at the blond woman. The young woman, who had been "dead" earlier in the day, was biting into a donut with relish.

"It all began about two years ago, when my grandfather moved into

Barnet Court," said Inspector Haddock. "At first, he was very happy with the place. He was delighted that he knew a few of the residents, especially Miss Eppel."

Miss Eppel blushed. "Sir Harold was from the old school," she explained. "He expressed gratitude for even the smallest bit of assistance. He was a gentleman."

"Then when Mr. Perlow and Mr. and Mrs. Bernfeld arrived, he had quite a nice circle of friends."

"We did have some good times at meals, swapping stories," said Ronny.

"Of course, Sir Harold was always very discreet," Rubles assured Inspector Haddock. "He never used real names when telling a story about Scotland Yard."

"Then he began to become uneasy, about some additions to his monthly bill," Inspector Haddock continued. "He was aware there would be occasional extra charges — a support bandage for a wrist that ached, special ointment for a rash, the need for an extra load of laundry, and things like that. But the cost of the items seemed to him to be much too high."

"When Sir Harold mentioned the problem to me," said Miss Eppel, "I began to take a closer look at my monthly bill, and I noticed the extra charges as well."

"My grandfather began to make discreet inquiries, but he couldn't come up with anything solid," continued Inspector Haddock. "Some of the residents didn't recall if they had ordered a special pillow for their neck, for instance. All they knew was that the pillow was on their bed one day. They hadn't questioned why the pillow cost a hundred pounds, because they hadn't looked closely at their bill. The money was deducted automatically from their bank account, and so they didn't notice."

"It was very wicked," said Miss Eppel, shaking her head.

"A few months before my grandfather passed away, Sir Harold asked if I could look into the matter. But there wasn't much I could do. He, like the other residents, had signed a form that allowed Barnet

Court to order medications, medical aids, and other services the person might need. If the person couldn't remember approving the expense — well, it was their word against the word of management. Because I had no real proof of fraud, I couldn't come in here officially and start snooping around. It was only when Miss Eppel mentioned that you were moving to Barnet Court, Mrs. Krinsky, I thought there might be a way to get inside."

"You took a very big risk, Inspector," said Miss Eppel. "I don't know if Sir Harold would have approved."

"I always say, when there's nowhere to go, go forward," said

Rubles.

"And when I followed your advice, I usually got coshed on the head," said Ronny.

"Perhaps that's why you still have all your marbles, dear. A good *klop* every once in a while may loosen up the dry rot."

"Perhaps I'm being regrettably dense, but where do I come into it?" asked Agatha.

"I wanted to see the papers that a new resident signed," said Inspector Haddock, "and you are the first new person to arrive in several months. You understand, I couldn't ask to see the papers without a plausible reason. I therefore had to invent the reason."

"A murder, you mean?" asked Agatha.

"That's right."

"So the whole thing — the body, the police surgeon and the rest of your staff — they were all putting on a show?" Agatha paused, to assimilate this new information. "It was very well done, Inspector. But how did you know I would get lost and enter the library and discover the body? It's not like this was a novel, and you could control the characters — although it often happened in my mystery novels that my characters would go off and do what they wanted, regardless of what I said."

"Actually, it's you, Mrs. Krinsky, who was the rebellious character."

Agatha looked surprised.

"You weren't supposed to discover the body until after lunch," Inspector Haddock continued. "I asked Miss Eppel to keep an eye on you this morning, and make sure you didn't sign anything before you arrived in the dining room. After lunch, she and the others were supposed to escort you to the library, where you would discover the body and Miss Eppel would call 'the police,' meaning me, immediately."

"I'm afraid I had to use the ladies room at the decisive moment," said Miss Eppel, blushing furiously. "By the time I returned to my station near Mrs. Krinsky's room, I saw she was already gone."

"But if this little charade was supposed to happen after lunch, whose body did I see this morning?" asked Agatha.

"That was my mistake," said the blond-haired young woman, whose name was Miss Brewster. "Or rather it was the mistake of my acting agency. They told me to show up at Barnet Court at eleven this morning and wait in the library, when the call really should have been for one. After about a half hour or so of lying on the carpet and pretending to be a corpse and wondering where everyone was, I got a cramp in my leg and had to stand up. I then decided to call my agency. They had assured me the job would take no more than an hour, and since I had an audition later in the afternoon I wanted to see what was going on. Then I heard the door handle move and I jumped back down onto the carpet."

"You did surprise us, Mrs. Krinsky, when you told us at lunch you had already discovered the body," said Miss Eppel. "We had to keep you in the dining room until the correct hour, the time that Inspector Haddock and his team would be waiting nearby. You must have thought us very unfeeling."

"I did find your apathy puzzling," Agatha admitted. She then turned to Inspector Haddock. "What exactly did you find in that folder of papers, Inspector? My nephew's wife, who is a lawyer, had looked through them before and Sheldon — that's my nephew — assured me it was fine for me to sign them."

"Oh, the Barnet Court papers were in order. But there was one document that had most likely been slipped into the folder after your family looked over the others. This is a copy of what I found. The original has been sent on to my office at the Yard, as evidence."

Inspector Haddock handed the paper to Agatha, who read it over.

"I'm afraid I don't see anything wrong."

"The change is very slight. It would take sharp eyes to see it. But if you look closely, you'll see that you're not authorizing Barnet

Court to remove funds from your bank account to cover additional expenses. You're authorizing an entity called Burnet Court."

"Who are they?" asked Agatha.

"I've got my staff working on that question now. If my suspicions are correct, I think we'll discover that Burnet Court is a company set up by Miss Carstairs and her associates."

"But if she was already cheating the residents and billing it to Barnet Court, why was there a need for a second company?"

"You see, dear," said Miss Eppel, "the extra charges were just to see if anyone would notice and make a fuss. If they did complain, which is what Sir Harold did, the extra charges stopped. But Sir Harold wasn't satisfied with that. He was concerned about the residents who weren't as alert as he was, or hadn't family close by to keep an eye on things. He therefore asked me to not say anything, to pretend I hadn't noticed anything amiss. A month later, I was no longer charged for extras I couldn't remember. Instead, money disappeared from my bank account for no reason at all."

"And presumably that money was going into the bank account of this Burnet Court," said Agatha. "Yes, I understand now."

"It was foolish of them to think they could pull the wool over your eyes, Miss Eppel," said Ronny.

"The Sandra Carstairs of the world don't realize a person has to pay attention to what she's doing when she crochets, or she'll miss a stitch and ruin the row," replied Miss Eppel. "Besides, as I mentioned at lunch, one rarely meets anyone named Carstairs in real life. When she joined the company and I was told her name, my suspicions were immediately aroused. I was sure that wasn't her real name and I said as much to Sir Harold."

"Yes, my grandfather mentioned that," said the Inspector. "I wouldn't be surprised if the young lady has a whole slew of aliases."

"It's a pity she was able to jump out the window and slip through your fingers," said Miss Brewster, who had finished her donut.

"We did that on purpose," he replied. "We want to see where she goes and who she contacts, while we're collecting the evidence against her. She won't get away with this."

"I hope not. You are all much too nice," Miss Brewster said to the others. She then stood up and shook the donut crumbs from her skirt. "I do need to be on my way, Inspector, if you don't need me anymore."

Inspector Haddock also rose from his chair. "Thank you, Miss Brewster. And I'm sorry we made you miss your audition."

"Oh, that's all right," she said. "I got a text message earlier that the play is going to close, so the audition was called off."

After Miss Brewster left the room, Rubles let out a sigh. "I wish there were more like her on the staff here," she said. "It's nice to see a young person who doesn't have a fake smile glued to her face."

"Sandra was the worst offender when it came to fake smiles," said Ronny. "I could kick myself for not realizing she wasn't on the level. But I really thought that if a crime were committed here, it would be done by our Maggie."

"That's because no money was taken from our account," said Rubles. "Sandra probably didn't want to risk it, since there were two of us to notice anything suspicious."

"What about you, Mr. P.?" asked Ronny. "Was Sandra dipping into your bank account?"

Monsieur Perlow smoothed down his hair. It bounced back up. "I noticed, here and there. I asked the questions. As the Inspector mentioned, the replies from Mademoiselle Carstairs seemed plausible. Yes, this was a tough olive to crack."

"Nut," said Rubles.

"Pardon?"

"The expression is that it's a tough nut to crack, Mr. P.," said Ronny.

Herschel Perlow raised his eyes heavenward. "How anyone can learn this English language of yours, *mes amis,* is a miracle."

If you enjoyed The Latke in the Library & Other Mystery Stories for Chanukah, *please consider leaving a review at your favorite online bookseller. Thanks so much!*

ABOUT THE AUTHOR

Libi Astaire is an award-winning author who often writes about Jewish history. In addition to her Jewish Regency Mystery Series set in early 19th-century London, she is the author of *Terra Incognita*, a novel about modern-day descendants of Spain's crypto-Jews, *The Banished Heart*, a novel about Shakespeare's writing of *The Merchant of Venice*, and several volumes of Chassidic tales. She lives in Jerusalem, Israel.

For updates about these and future books, visit her website at libi astaire.weebly.com.

The employees of Thorndike Press hope you have enjoyed this Large Print book. All our Thorndike, Wheeler, and Kennebec Large Print titles are designed for easy reading, and all our books are made to last. Other Thorndike Press Large Print books are available at your library, through selected bookstores, or directly from us.

For information about titles, please call:
(800) 223-1244

or visit our website at:
gale.com/thorndike

To share your comments, please write:
Publisher
Thorndike Press
10 Water St., Suite 310
Waterville, ME 04901